Montana Rancher's Kiss

Montana Rancher's Kiss

A Cole Brothers Romance

Kaylie Newell

TULE
PUBLISHING

Dedication

For Nola. I love you all the way to the bottom.

"See, when I flipped it, I didn't have the courage to do it the way I should've. But you can always pick it up, and if you're alone in the kitchen, who is going to see? But the only way you learn how to flip things is just to flip them."

-Julia Child

Prologue

D AISY HUDSON UNBUCKLED her seat belt with trembling hands as the passengers around her began standing to open their overhead bins. No matter how many times she'd rehearsed this day in her mind, it still hadn't prepared her for the actual moment. A sick stomach, an aching heart.

She glanced out the airplane's smudged window to the Montana mountain range in the distance. It looked like a row of monster's teeth, jagged and dark against the robin's egg sky. A sky so big, it was hard to comprehend. But it was those teeth that worried her. Looking like they were ready to chew her up and spit her out all over Marietta's picture-perfect Main Street.

She stood as the elderly woman who'd been sitting beside her shuffled into the aisle. She turned to Daisy and smiled, her cottony hair like a cloud on top of her head.

"Welcome home, honey."

Daisy smiled back, fighting tears. She wouldn't cry. *She would. Not. Cry.*

"Thank you," she said. "And have a nice time visiting

your son."

And then the woman was gone, lost in the crowd of passengers eager to debark the stuffy plane. Personally, Daisy was tempted to stay. She could ask the cheerful flight attendant for a blanket and a pillow, and then curl right back up in her seat for the next six months or so.

Instead, she took a deep breath and hoisted the leather carry-on over her shoulder. One of the things Alex had left in his side of the closet when he'd left. In those first few days, she'd sat on the couch and held it close to her chest. Thinking she could smell him in the fibers of the bag. A trace of his cologne, the faint scent of hotel soap. But then she'd gotten the call that her mother had died, and all that longing and despair had turned into a yawning chasm, and it had scared her. She needed to go home. To try and make things right, even if it was too late to fix the things that mattered most.

She stepped into the aisle in front of a soldier in fatigues who insisted she go first. She thanked him softly, trying to remember the color of her baby sister's eyes. Dark blue? Or were they brown? But the only thing she could picture with any clarity was Lily waving goodbye almost ten years ago now. Not quite out of high school yet, on the brink of making some hard decisions herself. But she'd ended up staying. Lily was all their mother had, and she wouldn't leave her. But Daisy had. God forgive her.

She stepped forward, gripping the handle of the bag so tightly that her nails bit into her palm. She'd left behind so many things that day, thinking that she'd finally conquered her childhood pain. But in reality, she'd only been running away from it. From her mother. From Brooks...

At the thought of the boy she'd fallen in love with at sixteen, her chin trembled.

"Have a nice day," the flight attendant said, her teeth flashing white against ruby-red lips. *Ruby-red slippers*, Daisy thought. *There's no place like home...*

She followed the line of people up the tunnel, the muted sounds of the Bozeman airport growing louder and more significant in her ears. Her heart tapped against her breastbone, reminding her of a hammer against glass. How long before it would break?

There was a throng of people near the gate. Waiting for their friends and loved ones. Daisy squinted through the bright, fluorescent lighting, looking for her sister in the crowd. She only knew what she looked like now from her Facebook pictures—a petite blonde with a megawatt smile and a pregnant belly.

Suddenly, there was a ridiculous urge to turn around and get back on the plane. To fly right back to Boston, to her life that was broken, but familiar. She didn't know if she could do this. She really didn't.

And then she saw Lily. She was standing behind a woman holding up a sign for someone named Lois. Lily stood on her tiptoes and craned her neck. And when she locked eyes with her only sibling, she smiled.

Brown, thought Daisy. *Of course they're brown.*

Chapter One

Save your bacon fat!

B ROOKS COLE STOPPED in front of the cat food display at Monroe's Market and pushed his Stetson back on his head. Elvira was fat enough. Did she really need something that boasted filet mignon on the label?

Without letting himself think too much about it, he reached out and grabbed a can, then two more, and tossed them into his cart. Whatever. She liked good food. Who could blame her?

He pushed the squeaky cart forward, checking one more thing off his mental list of groceries that he really should've written down. But to be fair, he wasn't used to this part of running the dude ranch. Since Charlie was facing back surgery, they'd be out a cook for the entire summer. He was going to have to get used to shopping until they could find a replacement. Which only made him want to rush this new hire even more. He hated grocery shopping. The only thing worse in his opinion, was worming the cattle.

The market was quiet this morning, with only the occasional shopper passing him in that friendly, albeit zoned-out way that grocery shoppers had. Every now and then a teenage boy with the cracking voice to match, announced another special over the loudspeaker. Today it was beef. Buy one pound, get half a pound free. Not bad. Brooks added stopping by the meat counter to his list.

"Well, Brooks Cole," a voice said behind him. "Fancy seeing you here."

He turned. And immediately wished he hadn't. Kylee Turner stood there, gripping her shopping cart like she was tempted to run him over with it. She wore tight jeans, and an even tighter western shirt which was trying its best to take his attention off the jeans. Her sleek brown hair hung in ripples past her shoulders, her long, dark eyelashes batting toward him like palm fronds.

She smiled, and Brooks braced himself. He knew that look. She was ready to spar, right here in Monroe's of all places.

"And on a Sunday morning, too," she said. "Shouldn't you be in church?"

He smiled back. "I do all my praying at the ranch. You know that."

"Uh huh."

"And why aren't you in church?"

"I just came from there. If you must know."

He glanced down at her shirt, which was gaping open to expose some very *non*-Sunday cleavage.

"I heard Charlie was down for the count," she continued, shaking her head. "Shame. That means you get to do all the shopping. And I know how much you hate that." She said this last part with a sparkle in her eyes. She actually loved anything that caused Brooks inconvenience. Or pain. Or discomfort in any way. They'd broken up a year ago, but she was still pissed at him. And rumor had it, wanted to get back together. That, he wasn't so sure about, since she was mean as a damn snake every time he ran into her.

"Yeah, well," he said in his best *whatever* drawl. It used to drive her crazy.

"Yeah well, *what?*"

He smiled wider, satisfied. He could still hit a nerve. "We've got an ad up for a temporary cook. So it won't be long."

She pursed her lips. Obviously, she'd been hoping he'd have to grocery shop until the end of time.

Jamming his thumb over his shoulder, he went on. "You know…judging by the interest we've gotten so far. There were lots of numbers torn off that flyer when I came in."

She shifted her gaze toward the bulletin board by the front door. "Well, I feel sorry for anyone who comes to work for you, Brooks. Since you're void of any kind of emotion. You treat that dumb cat better than the people in your life."

She'd never liked Elvira. One of the hundred reasons why they hadn't worked out. Well, that, and the fact that his heart had always belonged to someone else.

Kylee examined her nails and an awkward silence fell between them.

He felt kind of bad for needling her. Maybe he should apologize. Or say something nice about her outfit. Something to throw some water on this new fire he'd started. She was prickly as hell, but she was right—his relationships could use a little work.

She looked up and narrowed her eyes. Her green eyeshadow sparkled like stardust under the aisle five lighting. "Isn't that…"

Frowning, he turned. Standing in front of the bulletin board, was a woman wearing a white tank top and a pair of faded overalls. Her back was turned to them, her blond hair piled in a messy bun on top of her head. She was reaching for his flyer.

Brooks watched her. Wondering why she'd caught Kylee's attention like she had. He let his gaze settle on her bare shoulders. Her long, slender neck. The wisps of honey-colored hair tucked behind her ears. And something stirred inside him.

Kylee let out a soft sigh. "Oh my God…"

And then Brooks felt his back stiffen. His heartbeat slowed in his chest, a steady *thump, thump, thump*, that did nothing to move the blood through his veins. His hands were suddenly cold, his feet inside his boots, numb.

"She's got a lot of nerve coming back here," Kylee hissed.

He didn't answer. In fact, he probably couldn't if he'd

tried.

"I mean, after all this *time*?" Kylee looked over at him. He could feel the weight of her gaze, the meaning in it.

The woman in the overalls tucked the piece of paper from the flyer into her pocket. Then put her head down and walked out the door.

"She's got a lot of nerve, alright," Brooks said, pulling his Stetson low. "A hell of a lot of nerve."

Chapter Two

If in doubt, add a teaspoon of sugar.

D AISY GLANCED AT the address on the small scrap of paper sitting on the passenger seat. The ranch was so far out, her GPS wasn't working. Which wasn't great, because she was terrible at directions. The man on the phone had used north and south, when what she'd really needed was left and right. With a few landmarks thrown in for good measure. But she'd wanted to seem confident and capable, so she hadn't asked any more questions, which she absolutely should have. She couldn't be late for this interview.

She looked back up at the sprawling Montana landscape and shifted into fourth. It had been years since she'd driven a stick, and Lily's Jeep was old and clunky, the clutch working against Daisy's shaky foot instead of with it. But she was managing.

A gust of summer wind blew Daisy's hair across her face. It stuck to her lip gloss. She brushed it away again, wishing she'd at least worn it in a ponytail. The air smelled sweet, like animals and hay. The sun was golden and warm, but it would be hot later, blistering down on the rolling pastures and farmland like something on fire. She felt the beginnings of sweat trickling between her breasts, and knew that by noon, her cute sleeveless dress would be wilted. And so would she.

Leaning forward, she squinted at a driveway in the distance. It was flanked by two iron gates that were swung open like a pair of welcoming arms. A heavy wooden sign next to the road read *Diamond in the Rough Ranch.*

Daisy's stomach curled into a nervous ball as she shifted down and flipped on her blinker. The gravel road leading to the ranch was long and narrow, lined with big, shady oaks with gnarled, twisting limbs. Pastures stretched out on either side of her, with lazy, red-coated cattle grazing in them. A massive barn sat on the hill in the distance, a country queen on her dusty throne. Several log cabin-style buildings peppered the property, but the main house stole the show. It was lovely, and she knew from a quick Google search last night that it was old, too. She loved old things. Diamond in the Rough went back to the beginning of the 1900s and had been a working ranch for most of that time, except for a few misguided years in the '80s, when a new owner had tried to turn it into a restaurant.

Looking at it now, she felt like she'd stepped back in time. The log ranch house was a single story, sprawling structure with a wide front porch stretching all the way across. As Daisy got closer, she could see a couple of rocking chairs sitting out, waiting for the next contemplative souls to rest there. Colorful hanging baskets lined the overhang, still dripping from their morning watering, and there was a chunky wreath gracing the front door—something made of evergreen, which fit. Actually, everything about this property fit—the pastures, the cattle, the house and barn. They all fit together like pieces of a Montana puzzle, and all of a sudden, she felt a homesickness so complete, that it nearly stole her breath. She'd missed Marietta with a deep and painful ache that she'd learned to push down these last few years out of pure survival. Because she'd left. And she'd been too proud, too scared to come home again.

But now, here she was. Parking her sister's Jeep in the shade of a weeping willow and cutting the engine. Wearing a dress that she'd bought for a husband who, it turned out, had never really loved her. And mourning a mother she'd never really known.

She looked at her reflection in the rearview mirror and pulled in a breath. Telling herself that those were things that had happened to her. Not things that would define her. This was a new beginning. She kept repeating it, like a mantra inside her brain. *A new beginning, a fresh start. Mama would be proud of this...*

Squaring her shoulders, she grabbed her purse and pushed the Jeep door open, which groaned in protest. Her stomach churned. She'd worked hard in Boston but hadn't been on a payroll in years. Alex had made enough money for her to be able to focus on the volunteering that she loved so much. But mostly, he'd been anticipating her staying home with their family—children, which had never come to be. They'd tried for years, but she couldn't get pregnant. He hadn't blamed her, at least not out loud, but she'd always blamed herself. Just another thing they hadn't been able to get past. That, and the fact that he didn't want to adopt.

She looked up at the ranch house and smoothed down the white, eyelet material of her dress which didn't actually need smoothing. She knew she was going to have to sweet talk her way into this job. She'd been away from the market for too long, so her skillset was at a solid zero. Not to mention, Marietta was a small town with limited employment opportunities. At least for someone like her.

Tucking her purse underneath her arm, she walked across the gravel drive, trying not to turn her ankle in her strappy heels. She felt overdressed now that she was actually here, but she'd been nervous. She just wanted to get this right. She wanted this job. But more importantly, she needed this job.

She climbed the porch steps, her heels clicking hollowly over the old wood planks, and lifted her chin. Trying to summon some courage, some plucky, Marietta confidence. Since the opening at Diamond in the Rough was for a cook. And she and cooking had parted ways a long time ago.

She raised her fist and knocked with her heart pounding in her chest. The wreath on the door smelled like a Christmas tree. The screen windows on either side of her were open to let in the morning breeze, and after a few seconds, she could hear the heavy thudding of boots making their way toward the door. A deep voice telling someone named Elvira to scoot.

And then the door swung open, and Daisy felt the ridiculously wide smile on her mouth wilt like a thirsty flower.

She stared up at the man in front of her, and all of a sudden, her knees, which had been shaking before, felt like they were going to dump her in a white, eyelet puddle on the porch. All the color must have drained from her face, but the guy standing over her looked completely unconcerned. In fact, he leaned casually against the doorjamb, a cocky expression on his face. His hazel eyes were hard though, considering her with all the warmth of a wolf.

"Well, now," he said, running a hand through his dark hair, which had a serious hat ring around it. "Look who's back in town."

Daisy's mouth hung open. A plump black cat had sauntered out the open door and was now winding itself around her ankles, but she barely noticed.

He was taller than she remembered. And more rugged-looking. But that wasn't exactly a surprise, since the boy she'd left behind had long since grown into a man. His jaw was rough with stubble, his thick shoulders, giving way to an even thicker chest. He wore a blue plaid shirt, which did nothing to hide the muscle underneath. If anything, it accentuated it, the material stretching over his upper body in a way that would make most women sit up and take notice.

Despite her dizzy head, Daisy noticed, too. And the color that had probably been missing from her cheeks before, flooded back with a rush of heat.

"Brooks…" It was the only thing she could manage. She hadn't said that name out loud in almost a decade.

"Daisy," he answered back. His voice, on the other hand, was smooth as scotch.

"I didn't know…I didn't realize…"

His jaw worked back and forth. "How could you? You've been gone all this time, remember?"

"Do you work here?" If she'd run the specifics of this interview by Lily, her sister would've probably been able to warn her. But she'd wanted to do this on her own. Lily had enough to worry about as it was.

He smiled, but his eyes were flinty. "I own the place. With Porter."

Porter. Another name she hadn't allowed herself to think about in years. Brooks's fraternal twin brother whom he'd been so close with in high school. They'd had a younger brother, too. Griffin. Their famous dad had sent them all to Marietta to live with an aunt as pre-teens. Details that as a girl hadn't been as important as the color of his eyes, which always seemed to change with the light.

He pushed off the doorjamb and stuck his hands in the pockets of his Wranglers. Without meaning to, she let her gaze fall to his big silver belt buckle. His trim waist. His thick wrists, which looked strong and capable. Brooks had always been strong, though. His body might've changed, but the person inside was probably the same. And her heart gave a painful lurch.

"And can I ask why you're gracing us with your presence today?" he asked flatly.

Okay. She deserved that. She'd known when she left Boston that she was going to have to eat a certain amount of crow when she got home. She just didn't think it was going to be so soon. And served up by her childhood boyfriend to boot.

She stared up at him. "The job. For a cook? I'm here for an interview."

He laughed—a deep, throaty laugh, that stung. He wasn't going to make this easy. But she was at his mercy, here. She had to do her best to deflect whatever he was going to throw at her. And he'd throw plenty, if that laugh was any indication. The unwelcome thought that she was a dismal cook on a good day tickled the back of her mind again, but she shoved it away. He didn't have to know that. In fact, he *wasn't* going to know if she could help it.

She stiffened her spine, telling herself not to be too un-done by those eyes. "What's so funny?"

"Nothing. Just the fact that you're wanting a job. From me of all people."

She watched him.

"And you know this is a live-in position?"

Yes, she'd known, but hadn't thought too much about it. And now that tiny detail seemed like the Mt. Everest of oversights.

She touched the diamond stud in her earlobe, a nervous habit. Then realized her hand was shaking and dropped it quickly to her side again. "Yes, I know."

"How long are you planning on staying? Or are you going to get homesick for the city and leave mid-summer?"

He was chucking everything in his arsenal at her, but she wasn't fooling herself into thinking he'd even gotten to the good stuff yet. She had no idea how much he knew about her current situation but had to assume he knew plenty.

"I'm not going to leave," she said. "I have nothing to go back to."

If she'd expected sympathy, which she hadn't, she would've been disappointed. He watched her coolly, his expression unreadable. He made no move to invite her in for the interview. But he hadn't told her to leave, either, which she took as a good sign. Brooks Cole didn't have to love her. He didn't even have to like her. He just needed to hire her.

"Mama died," she said. She hadn't meant to get into all that, but it had just popped out. And after it did, a painful lump settled in her throat. She swallowed it down, along with her pride, and hoped they'd stay put.

"I know. I'm sorry."

The cat rammed its head against her ankle. Daisy glanced

down and smiled, despite herself. It looked up through eyes the color of lemon wedges and meowed hoarsely. She longed to pick it up and hold its warm, squishy body against her face. Alex had been allergic to cats.

"That's Elvira," Brooks said. "She runs the place. For all intents and purposes."

The cat meowed again, then sat on her haunches and began licking a dainty paw.

From somewhere across the ranch, a horse whinnied. The sound echoed over the rolling pastures. The breeze made the wind chimes on the porch tinkle delicately, bringing with it Brooks's clean scent. And Daisy's toes curled.

He narrowed his eyes at her. "You really want this job?"

Her heartbeat kicked up a notch, but she was afraid to get too excited. "I really do."

"Then you're going to have to interview for it, just like everyone else."

"Of course."

The exchange was stiff and awkward, but it was something.

"Don't thank me. I haven't offered it to you yet." He stepped aside and motioned for her to come inside.

Dipping her head, she brushed past, trying to ignore his physical proximity. He reminded her of a tiger, contemplating her like dinner.

She looked up at the spacious room she found herself standing in and let out a breath. It was beautiful. The log house was rustic enough on its own, but whoever had been in charge of decorating it had hit the dude-ranching nail on the head. The couches were upholstered in dark, studded leather, and were accented by heavy, natural wood chairs. The southwestern print area rug added a splash of color and drew the attention toward the massive fireplace on the other side of the room. Smooth, round river rock made up the mantel, where a pair of sun-bleached antlers hung.

"Sit," Brooks said. "Please." He motioned toward one of the chairs.

She did as she was told, and eased herself down, too nervous to get comfortable. She took a deep breath. The house smelled like saddle leather and bacon, and her heart fluttered unexpectedly.

He sat opposite her. "So," he said, clasping his hands in front of his belt buckle. "Where should we start?"

She watched him. And all of a sudden, the image of him in the bed of his old Ford pickup hung behind her eyes. Shirtless and tan, his face as smooth as the Marietta River in July. She saw him reach for her. She remembered being angry and pushing him away. If she could go back and let him touch her, would she? Would she actually let him reach her? She didn't know. Maybe she'd never know.

She blinked, holding her purse to her stomach. "I'm sorry. What?"

"Why don't you tell me a little about yourself? Since it's been so long…"

If he wanted to make her squirm, he was doing a great job. The trick was not letting him *see* her squirm. She relaxed into the chair and forced a smile.

"Well, I've been living in Boston for the last nine years. I'm newly divorced..."

His dark brows rose at that.

"And how's Alex doing?" he asked. Looking very much like he hoped his former best friend had been hit by a bus.

"He's fine. We haven't really talked lately. He's in Hong Kong for work."

Brooks nodded. "Does he know you came back?"

"He knows."

"Does he care?"

Another strategic arrow to the heart. Alex cared, but she understood how other people might not see it that way. It had taken her a long time to figure him out, and to accept that caring and loving were two different things. He'd sent flowers when her mother had died and had been uncharacteristically warm when asking about her plans to come home to Marietta. His tone had bordered on nostalgic, which had thrown her off. Alex didn't really do nostalgia.

Brooks must've noticed the expression on her face, because he looked away for a second. When he looked back, his eyes were softer. Not much, but a little.

"And what did you do in Boston?" he asked. "To qualify you for this job?"

"Well, I volunteered at a soup kitchen for the homeless."

She'd served the soup. She'd never cooked it. Small detail.

"You know your way around a kitchen then."

It was a statement, not a question. So she nodded, convincing herself it wasn't as much of a fib to just agree. "My mom was a wonderful cook," she said. "I grew up watching her. Well...you already knew that."

Her mother *had* been a wonderful cook. She'd even owned a small restaurant for a few years. Lou Hudson had insisted that her daughters work there on the weekends and after school, and Daisy had been happy to do it because it meant more time together. But no matter how hard she tried to learn, to please her mom, she never could. The constant criticism, the feeling of never measuring up or being good enough, had taken its toll on a girl desperate for her only parent's approval. Until Daisy grew to associate cooking with failure and loss.

Yet, here she was.

"Anything else on your resume?"

She shook her head. "No. But I loved working at the kitchen. And I was good at it." Boston had been dark in so many ways, but her time at St. Nicholas was a bright spot. It had taught her tenderness and love. Things that she'd craved and hadn't understood existed outside the gruffness of her mother, and the dismissiveness of her husband. She'd found love in Boston. Just not the kind she'd expected.

The cat, Elvira, jumped into her lap and immediately began making biscuits on her thighs. Daisy laughed, happy with the distraction, which had come at the perfect time. Thinking about her mother rarely ended well.

"Elvira, no." Brooks got up and nudged her off. She hopped down with a significant thud and glared back at him.

"It's okay. Really."

"She'll shed all over you."

"Well, if I end up working at a ranch, I'll have to get used to a little animal hair."

She said this with a smile, but he didn't smile back. Instead, his gaze lingered on her dress, as if it were snagged there.

He cleared his throat. "Why don't I show you the kitchen."

Standing, she tucked her purse under her arm and followed him across the house. She tried to keep her own gaze locked on the back of his head like a good job applicant, but it fell to his butt anyway. He'd always had a nice backside. Especially in Wranglers.

They stepped into the kitchen and she glanced around, trying to pay attention now, since this was where she might be spending her summer. Like the living room, it was huge. A neat row of brass pots and pans hung over the stainless-steel oven. The big picture window, topped with a red gingham valance, looked out onto the pastures and barn in the distance. The light in here was soft and warm, bathing the tiled countertop in butter yellow. It was a country kitchen, functional, and made for cooking large meals, but it was also sweet and welcoming, and she found herself wanting to sit down at the island and have a cup of coffee.

"Charlie's been our cook for years," Brooks said, leaning against fridge. "So this job's only temporary. Only for the summer."

She nodded. "I understand. Can I ask why?"

"She's having surgery."

"She?"

"Charlie's a she."

"Oh…I just assumed…"

"Never assume around here. This ranch will eat you alive." He said this last part like he might be looking forward to that a little.

She looked over at the pots and pans, hanging expectantly on their heavy hooks, and felt mildly sick. Maybe this ranch *would* eat her alive. And then what? She was officially out of options.

She turned around for a second and ran her hands over the countertop, mostly, so he wouldn't see her collect herself. When she turned back, she smiled. "It seems quiet this morning. Are there guests here now?"

"There's a family from Idaho, and some newlyweds from Helena. Porter has them out riding. They'll be in for lunch."

"That seems like a manageable group."

He smiled slowly. "We haven't hit our busy season yet. Which is July and August. Cooking for that many people is tough."

She nodded.

"And of course, there's the grocery shopping."

She nodded again.

"And the cleanup. A dozen people can make a big mess."

She thought of the time an angry pre-teen at St. Nicholas had flung his lunch, his mother's lunch, *and* his sister's lunch against the wall. Daisy had found bits of celery in the heating vents days later. She knew how to clean up.

"The cook has a small room on the second floor," he continued. "Nothing fancy. And I know you're used to fancy."

"I'm really not."

"Alex promised you the moon, remember? *And* the stars?" His hazel eyes were chilly, but his handsome face hurt her heart. If he looked this good mad, she could only imagine how he'd look agreeable.

"He may have promised me the moon, Brooks, but he didn't exactly deliver."

"Huh. Well, I could've told you that."

He'd been turned inside out when they'd broken up. And then she'd married his best friend. His anger was justified. She'd been angry at herself for a long time, too. If telling her *I told you so* was what was going to help him work through it, that was okay. She could take it. Maybe it would help her work through some of it, too.

She chewed the inside of her cheek for a second, trying to think of something to say. Nothing seemed to fit. Her pulse tapped out a steady rhythm in her wrists, making her more than aware of her body's reaction to Brooks Cole. He'd always had this effect on her. It was one of the reasons she'd wanted them to get married right after high school. He made her feel alive. She wanted him for her own; she'd wanted *something* for her own. And when he couldn't make her the promises she longed for, she'd turned to someone else.

It was only now, standing here in the kitchen of his beautiful ranch house, that she began to see how young they'd really been. And that his only example of parenthood, like hers, had been turbulent. Having a father who'd made so many mistakes, had made Brooks determined not to make the same ones. Daisy had been a casualty of that fear.

A door across the house opened, then slammed. She heard a pair of boots thudding across the living room floor, but kept her gaze on Brooks, unable to look away.

"Brooks!" a booming voice called. "Where's the cooler?"

A tall man entered the kitchen, a dusty cowboy hat riding low over his eyes. "I can't find the damn thing, and I've got thirsty people out here…"

His voice trailed off when he saw her. He swiped his hat off and pinched the brim between his fingers. He stood a few yards away, but she could smell the tangy scent of horse and sweat coming off him. Surprisingly pleasant. And appropriate, given their surroundings. This was a dude ranch, but it was also a working ranch, and she was being reminded of that with every passing minute.

"Ma'am."

Her heartbeat slowed in her chest as recognition set in. Brooks wasn't the only one who'd grown. His twin brother had changed, too.

"Porter?"

A gradual smile spread across his mouth. "Daiz?"

She grinned as he stepped forward and wrapped her in a bear hug. He lifted her up until her feet dangled over the kitchen floor. He smelled like ranch, alright, and was as warm as he was solid. They'd always gotten along well. Porter was the yin to Brooks's yang, and whenever she'd needed relationship advice, she'd come to him. But most of all, Daisy had just liked being around Porter. He was fun. And it didn't look like he was holding a grudge, which made her happy.

He set her down and held her at an arm's length. "Let me get a look at you," he said, shaking his head. "Still pretty as a picture. Maybe even prettier."

Her face warmed. Brooks was taking this all in from where he stood on the other side of the kitchen. He hadn't moved an inch, except to cross his arms over his chest. He was glaring at them both.

"Isn't she pretty?" Porter asked, glancing over at his brother, then looking back at her without waiting for an answer. Which was a good thing, because if the expression on Brooks's face was any indication, he'd be waiting a while.

"What in God's name are you doing here?" Porter asked,

still smiling. He was as good-looking as Brooks. But in a different way. Porter was the all-American boy next door. Easy smile, crinkles radiating from his friendly, green eyes. Brooks, on the other hand, just smoldered from the inside out. But maybe that had more to do with her than his general aura these days.

She smoothed a hand over her dress. "Well, Mama…"

"I heard about that. I'm so sorry."

She nodded. "Lily's going to have a baby this summer, and her husband is deployed. I came back to help. And…" She swallowed hard, wondering if she should say anything else. But honestly, the camaraderie felt nice. It had been a long time since anyone had asked her about herself. "I came back to try and make things right."

Brooks coughed from across the room.

"With Lily," Daisy added quickly. "And Mama's memory. If that's possible."

"It's possible," Porter said. "You need to make your peace with it."

She watched him, thankful for the kindness. She'd expected… Well, she didn't know what she'd expected, exactly. But this wasn't it. This felt like love. It felt like forgiveness.

Porter raised his brows. "Wait a minute. Did you come out here for the job?"

"I did."

Porter grinned and looked over at his brother again. "Well…what do you know."

"Yeah," Brooks mumbled. "What do you know."

"You gonna give her the job, brother?"

An awkward silence fell over the room, as the rooster clock above the oven clicked off the seconds like a bomb.

"I'm sure you have other applicants to consider," Daisy said. "I'll just get out of your hair…"

Brooks looked at the worn leather watch on his wrist. "I've gotta go meet Dad out at the shop anyway. I didn't realize how late it was."

"Your dad is visiting?"

"He's back," Brooks said evenly.

Daisy stared at him. "To stay?"

"Looks like you're not the only one wanting to make a change."

Brooks and Porter's father was a rock star who'd record-ed a Christmas song in the '90s that had made his debut album go platinum. His career had been launched into the stratosphere, and he'd thrived on the West Coast, but his family hadn't. He'd sent his boys to Marietta to live with his sister, and they'd ended up settling in like they'd been born here. But never in a million years would she have thought Eddie would come to Montana, too.

She smiled, warmed through. She knew how much Brooks and his brothers had missed him. At least when they'd been kids. "I'm so happy for you all," she said. "Really."

Porter smiled back, but Brooks continued watching her

quietly. Maybe he was remembering. She knew that since she'd laid eyes on him again, remembering was all she seemed to want to do.

"Thanks," he said. "I'll walk you out."

Chapter Three

Hold a piece of bread between your teeth when cutting onions. It'll stop the tears.

D AISY SAT ON the porch swing, watching Lily rub circles on her belly. Her little sister had her swollen feet propped up on a wicker ottoman, and kept wiggling her painted toes, which reminded Daisy of the cutest little sausages. Of course, she'd never say that out loud.

Looking at Lily, she felt another rush of affection. And shame. She never should've stayed gone this long. Never.

She stood and grabbed the pitcher of iced tea to refill her sister's glass. The ice cubes tinkled merrily, floating in harmony with thin slices of lemon. It was their mother's famous sun tea, and it tasted like summer itself. It reminded Daisy of the good things, of the sweet things, that were usually overshadowed by the bitter.

Sitting down again, she took a sip from her own glass. The afternoon was hot, but not too hot. A big box fan whirred from across the porch, and she leaned her head back and closed her eyes.

"You can't just leave it at that," Lily said. "You have to tell me everything."

Daisy kept her eyes closed, swinging gently. "That was it, mostly. He just asked a few questions about my qualifications, and then said he'd call me."

"After all these years," Lily said. "That must've been the shock of a lifetime."

"For me, or him?"

"For both of you."

At that, Daisy opened her eyes again and looked at her sister. "He's still mad at me."

"Well, yeah."

"I mean, I knew I'd run into him eventually. And I knew he'd be mad. And he has every right to be…"

"But it still hurts."

Daisy took another sip of tea, then licked the sweetness from her lips. "Yeah," she said. "I guess it does."

Lily glanced across the street toward some kids who were tossing a football back and forth. Their laughter echoed through the neighborhood.

"I was mad at you for a long time, too," she said, looking back at Daisy. "I'm sorry I never took your calls. I think I was jealous that you left. Resentful because of my own relationship with Mama… But I've missed you."

Daisy swallowed hard. Afraid she'd say something wrong. Then she put her glass down and got up to go sit by her sister.

"I was messed up for a long time, Lily," she said quietly. "I felt invisible at home, like I didn't matter. And the more I tried to love her, the more she pushed me away. Then Brooks… I just ran. It was the only thing I knew how to do. I'm so sorry I did that to you."

Without saying anything, Lily reached for her hand and squeezed it.

And there it was again—the forgiveness Daisy didn't think she deserved. Despite trying to blink them back, the tears came anyway. They spilled down her cheeks, and she wiped them away with the backs of her knuckles. It was funny. She'd never cried when Alex left. She'd barely cried when her mom died, even though the news had broken her in half. It had taken coming back to Marietta, and holding her little sister's hand, to make her feel safe enough to cry.

Letting go, Lily reached up to wipe her own eyes. "I still can't believe it, though."

"Believe what?"

"That this job is for a cook. You hate cooking."

"I always wanted to love it, though," Daisy said. "I wanted to be just like Mama. And then, I don't know. I could never figure out how to make her happy. And then I didn't want to make her happy anymore…"

Daisy looked away, lost in thought. Picturing their mother at her old stove, her favorite red apron tied snug around her waist.

"She was tough," Lily said. "I've never known anyone

tougher to get along with than Mama. But she loved you. She was just awful at showing it."

Daisy didn't answer. That was the understatement of the century. There were times over the years when she'd wondered if she'd been loved at all. And that's all she'd ever wanted. Alex had known that and had used it to get her to marry him. But she couldn't blame him for leaving Marietta. That was on her. And now, she was going to have to untangle this mess in her heart and figure out how to move forward.

"In fact," Lily said, getting up with a grunt. "I have something for you."

"Whatever it is, I can get it. Just tell me where it is."

Lily waved her away as she waddled over to the screen door. "You're spoiling me too much. I'm going to forget how to do anything for myself."

"If Jack were here, he'd be spoiling you. You deserve it."

Lily gave her a look over her shoulder. "You can spoil me by changing diapers."

Her little sister let the screen door slam behind her, and Daisy waited for a minute before Lily reappeared holding a book in her arms. She walked back over and sat down beside Daisy.

"Here you go."

Daisy stared down at the cookbook in her lap. Her mother's ancient copy of the *Joy of Cooking*. It was falling apart. There were handwritten recipes spilling out the sides.

Sticky notes marking pages, dog-eared and yellowed recipes that had been clipped from magazines. The whole thing must've weighed fifty pounds. Or maybe that was the weight of the expectation on her shoulders.

"It was Mama's favorite," Lily said, touching the worn cover. "And she wanted you to have it."

Daisy looked over at her sister. "What?"

"She told me last year. She'd been keeping it for you."

It was hard to absorb the words. The meaning of them. Daisy had always assumed her mother never thought about her after she'd left. *Out of sight, out of mind!* That's what she'd yelled at her oldest daughter after she'd announced she was moving to Boston. *Go ahead and go, but don't expect anyone to be pining away from here.*

You've never pined before, Mama, she'd answered back. *Why start now?*

Daisy remembered every detail of that fight. Every word hurled, every hurt inflicted. But now, with the weight of the cookbook on her lap, she remembered the tears in her mother's eyes as she'd turned away. There had been tears.

Shaking her head, she opened the cookbook to a random page. Cakes and pies. There was a sentence written out at the top of the page in her mother's neat handwriting. *Tip!* it said. *Cut cheesecake with a warm knife!*

There was a loose recipe card that had been tucked between the pages. *Grandma Irene's Apple Crisp.* Daisy's heart squeezed as she picked it up. Her memories of her grandmother were sparse. She'd died relatively young, leaving her daughter, whom she'd been close to, with no family at all. Just another deep pain inflicted in her mom's life.

Daisy remembered being hugged by her grandma, being held against her soft, squishy bosom. She remembered how she smelled, like cookies. She remembered that her gray hair stuck out in tufts above her ears. And she remembered that she'd loved to cook and had taught Daisy's mom everything she knew.

"Oh my goodness," Lily said. "Remember that apple crisp? I tried to make it once, and it turned out so soggy I had to throw it out."

The only apple anything that Daisy had eaten since, was whatever she'd bought in the freezer aisle. She and Alex had subscribed to a meal delivery service shortly after they'd gotten married. Her attempts at cooking had been a sad spectacle, and her heart hadn't been in it. Every time she stepped up to her big stainless-steel oven in their apartment, all she'd been able to think about was her mother. And then she'd picked up the phone and ordered takeout.

She tucked the recipe card back inside and closed the cookbook, careful not to let any of the loose clippings fall out.

"Mama always made it on July 4th, remember?" Daisy said. "We'd eat outside and watch the fireworks from the yard."

"And Mrs. Pickleseimer's dog would jump over the fence

and beg from our plates."

Daisy laughed. "Remember that time he ate an entire banana cream pie? Mama was so mad. I don't think she ever got over it."

"Mama? Never."

"To be fair, Mrs. Pickleseimer was her archrival, so…"

"Well, it was because they entered the same bake-off one Christmas. Mama came in second, and Mama *never* came in second. So I don't think it was the dog eating the pie, so much as it was *Mrs. Pickleseimer's* dog that ate the pie."

Daisy wiped her eyes. She hadn't cried from laughter in a long time. It felt so good, that for a second it was like going back—to when she and her sister had sat on their beds and gossiped about school friends and boys they thought were cute. She still remembered how Brooks had looked on the first day of sixth grade, tall and lanky for his age, a dark mop of hair falling over one eye. She'd taken one look and lost her heart.

Lily cradled her belly and put her feet back up on the ottoman. "I need to get ready for work pretty soon. Do you need the Jeep for anything before I go?"

Daisy shook her head. "I wish you didn't have to work this late in your pregnancy."

"I don't mind it. I love being at the library. It's cool in there and it smells like books."

A few strands of Lily's dark blond hair had escaped her ponytail and moved across her face in the breeze. She and her sister had the same color hair, only Daisy's was longer now. She'd need to find someone to cut it soon. It was hot and heavy on the back of her neck, but Brooks had always loved it long. She had no idea why that would matter anymore. It didn't.

"When are you supposed to hear back on the job?" Lily asked, taking a sip of her tea.

"Soon," she said. "Lord help me."

Chapter Four

Clean up as you go.

B ROOKS MADE HIS way across the pasture with Griffin stepping carefully beside him. His little brother was trying to avoid the freshest cow patties like the obsessive, slightly compulsive accountant that he was, but wasn't having much luck. Every now and then he'd utter a colorful cuss word or two under his breath.

Porter's dog ran up ahead, barking his head off. There really wasn't anything to bark at, but that didn't matter. Brooks figured it just felt good to bark. They were supposed to be inspecting the fence line along the river for any wear or damage, but Brooks was too preoccupied to pay much attention to anything. Especially fences that may or may not be needing repairs.

Glancing over at Griffin, he stopped in the shade of a giant spruce and rubbed the back of his neck. His brother wasn't much of a cowboy, bless him. But he did the books for Diamond in the Rough and visited often—drinking beer on the porch in the evenings and having Sunday dinners with the ranch hands and guests.

Griffin pushed his dark-framed glasses up, before waving a fly away. "Damn, it's hot."

"And gonna get hotter." Brooks looked over at the river, winding cool and lazy through its swath of emerald-green pasture. Before he could help it, he thought of the time he and Daisy had gone swimming in their underwear on a day so hot, it had hurt to breathe. They'd swung on an old tire that someone had hung from a weeping willow, its branches tickling the surface of the water like elegant fingers. He'd never forgotten how beautiful Daisy had looked, her hair slicked back from her face, beads of water clinging to her tan skin like diamonds.

"Brooks."

He stared at the river, barely registering his name. Or the fact that his brother had uttered it twice now.

"Yeah…"

"You should hire her."

At that, he looked back at Griffin, his jaw muscles tight.

"I mean, why not," Griffin continued. "It's water under the bridge. You were kids, for God's sake. And she probably needs the job."

"I doubt that. I'm sure she's got plenty of alimony." Then again, the Daisy he'd known had been stubborn. And proud. And Alex was an ass, who might not have made sure she was taken care of after their divorce. Maybe she really did need the job. Why else would she be applying for something as non-glamourous as this?

But when it all came down to it, he didn't know if he was ready to forgive her. He sure as shit didn't think he was ready to have her living in his house. Yes, it had been a long time. But there was a limit to what he could do. And watching her walk up the porch steps yesterday had nearly ripped his heart out of his chest.

He gazed over at the cattle grazing in the distance before looking at his brother again. "You forget this is a live-in job," he said evenly. "That could get really complicated, really fast."

Griffin nodded, hooking his thumbs in his beltloops. He'd been dating a woman for the last six months who owned a café over by the hospital and seemed to be settling into the couple life seamlessly. Unlike Porter and Brooks, who avoided any kind of serious relationship like the plague. Growing up with a rock star father who kept getting burned by people over and over again, did that to you. And then along came Daisy, who'd taken any kind of trust Brooks did have, and ripped it to shreds.

"I'm just saying," Griffin said, his voice low. "Charlie's going to be down for the count pretty soon, and you don't have as many people lining up for the job as you were hoping."

"True. But I have my doubts about whether she could even handle it. You know how hard it is. Charlie makes it look easy, but it's not."

"The Daisy I used to know could handle anything."

"The Daisy I used to know could, too. But she's different. She's changed. She's…"

Griffin's mouth tilted slightly. "She's what?"

"She's a pain in my ass."

"Just by growing up? Just by coming back here?"

"Exactly. Just by coming back here."

"You think that's fair?"

He shot his brother a look. "Whose side are you on, anyway?"

"Yours. But I remember how you used to feel about this girl."

"Well, I remember she ran off with my best friend."

"*After* you broke up."

A distinctive heat marched up Brooks's neck. Yeah, they'd broken up. But he'd still loved her. Just because they hadn't been able to decide on a future together, didn't make it okay to marry Alex. And, yeah. Maybe if Brooks hadn't been so dead set against settling down, maybe things would've been different for them. But he wasn't going to worry about that anymore. He hadn't been ready. And the fact that maybe he *never* would've been ready didn't matter. She hadn't stuck around to find out.

"I'm just saying," Griffin said, taking his glasses off, and rubbing them with the hem of his T-shirt. One of their dad's old tour shirts from the '90s. "Maybe she could use a break."

Brooks grunted, then picked up a stick and threw it toward the river. Clifford, Porter's border collie, appeared out of nowhere and caught it mid-air. He landed gracefully and trotted back toward Brooks, looking pleased with himself.

"Good boy," Brooks said.

The dog dropped the stick at his feet, then stood back to wait for another throw. His little body hummed with anticipation. Brooks obliged, this time chucking the stick a country mile. It landed with a plop in the river, and the dog launched himself after it. There was a border collie-shaped splash, and after a second, Clifford resurfaced with the damn thing in his teeth. He paddled back to the grassy riverbank, climbed out, and shook himself off. Water droplets went flying, a prism of rainbow colors underneath the warm afternoon sun.

Brooks watched, thinking of all the time he and Daisy had spent along this river as kids. Those had been good days. Simpler days. Now that they'd grown up, things were a hell of a lot more complicated. Should he give her a break and hire her? She was probably lying through her teeth about being a good match for this job. She used to loathe cooking. But those big brown eyes could sway anyone. Even an old boyfriend who'd kind of like to see her fall flat on her face.

Putting his hands in his pockets, he waited for Clifford to come back. Then felt a smile tug at the corner of his mouth. It might be kind of fun watching Daisy struggle with this if she *had* been exaggerating her skills. He guessed he could do both—be a semi-decent guy, and give her the break she needed. While simultaneously hoping she fell flat on her face.

He never said he was an angel.

DAISY STROLLED DOWN Main Street in the dusky, evening light, watching the old-fashioned streetlamps begin to wink on. She'd only meant to walk to Monroe's for Lily's favorite peanut butter cookies, but the cool air had felt so good after the heat of the day, that she'd kept on going.

She held the bag in her hand now, the crinkly plastic brushing against her bare leg as she passed the charming storefronts that had barely changed over the years. The small town where she'd grown up looked like it belonged in a snow globe, or better yet, in a Normal Rockwell painting. Even the people she passed on the sidewalk were a sight for sore eyes, their friendly smiles welcoming her home again. So far she'd seen an old high school teacher, her mother's quilting friend, and a little girl she used to babysit for, who was now going to the community college over in Bozeman.

She'd been nervous about coming into town for the first time, knowing she'd run into people. But nobody seemed to be judging her for leaving the way she had. At least not to her face.

Passing the Java Café, she breathed in the smell of warm bread and glanced over at the pharmacy, hoping she wouldn't see Carol Bingley, the owner. She remembered Carol as being nice, but exceptionally nosy, and knew that being cornered by her would mean reciting a complete rundown of her time in Boston, including, but not limited to, her divorce. Daisy picked up her pace, but immediately slowed again when she saw the sign for Mistletoe Music up ahead.

Her heart thumped heavily inside her chest. Lily had filled her in about the music shop that Brooks's dad had opened in Marietta. The shop was apparently a huge success, with people coming far and wide hoping to catch a glimpse of their childhood idol. Daisy had always loved the guitar, Eddie's favorite instrument, so she'd been a fangirl herself. But she'd only met him once, when he'd come out for Griffin's birthday one year. She'd been careful about talking about Eddie too much around Brooks, because all the Cole boys had been sensitive about his fame. They'd never known who wanted to be friends with them because of who they were, or who their father was. Daisy couldn't have cared less. She would've loved Brooks no matter what his father did for a living. But she knew there'd always been a part of him that hadn't believed that. He'd just had a hard time trusting— part of what had led to their breakup. He couldn't trust her, and his trust and love were all she'd ever wanted. A match made in hell.

She walked up to the shop window, gazing at the beautiful, glossy guitars in their display cases. The lights were soft inside the historic brick building that reminded her of old Westerns and cowboys that held the door open for you. There was a small sign next to a cherry-red Gibson that said, *Sign up for lessons inside!* Daisy had always wanted to learn how to play. She remembered listening to her mom's favorite country artists as a kid—Trisha Yearwood, Tim McGraw, The Judds, and secretly thinking that if she wasn't going to become the kind of cook her mom could be proud of, she could always learn to play the guitar.

Of course, that had never happened. She'd left town before she could ever figure her mother out. Much less make her proud.

Taking a breath, she ignored all the reasons why taking lessons of any kind right now wasn't very practical, except maybe if they were cooking lessons, and walked over to the front door to pull it open. She was met with a cool blast of air and looked up to see three giant ceiling fans circulating above her. A teenage boy squeezed by on his way out and muttered an apology. The entire place smelled like varnished wood and had a vintage warehouse feel to it. Expensive-looking guitars, ukuleles, and banjos lined the brick walls. Some painted in vibrant colors and designs, while others boasted their natural honey color and were just as striking. Mixed in with the instruments on the walls, were framed albums and awards. Daisy squinted up at a glass shadow box with what looked like an MTV Video Music Award in it. She recognized the iconic silver moon man with the flag, and immediately wondered what she was doing here. It was ridiculous. She wasn't a musician. She wasn't a cook. She wasn't even a Mariettan anymore. She felt like an imposter, trying to come back to a life that wasn't even hers.

Turning on her heel, she headed for the door.

"Not leaving already, are you?"

She stopped in her tracks and looked toward the sound of the low, gravelly voice coming from the top of the staircase. There, in a pair of black leather pants and a purple satin shirt open to the middle of his chest, was Eddie Cole. *The* Eddie Cole. The one with the MTV Video Music Award. The one with the platinum albums on the walls. The one with the son who now hated her, and who looked very much like his father in this light.

"I…" She was actually speechless.

He walked down the stairs, tall and lean in a pair of black biker boots. A couple of leather cuffs graced his wrists, and his signature shaggy blond hair brushed his shoulders, even though it looked to be thinning a little on top. She instantly understood his level of fame, his extraordinary success at the height of his career. He simply oozed confidence and sex appeal. He was a rock star through and through. No wonder Brooks had struggled with it. She couldn't imagine having a father like Eddie Cole. Of course, she couldn't imagine having a father at all. Her own dad had taken off when she and Lily were still drinking from sippy cups. She only had a hazy memory of someone lifting her over their shoulders once. She thought that was her father.

Glancing at a chunky silver watch on his wrist, Eddie shook his head. "Not closing up shop for another ten minutes or so." He looked at her and smiled, flashing straight white teeth against tanned skin. "Still time to buy a guitar. Or two."

Daisy smiled back, trying to remember how to act like a functional human being. Yes, this was Eddie Cole. But this close, she could also see a small razor nick next to his ear, which made her feel a little better. He was human, too.

"Oh, I'm not here to buy one," she managed, tightening her grip around the bag of cookies. "I'm just browsing. I don't even play."

He stepped toward her. "Shame. Everyone should play. Of course, that's only my opinion, but you know…"

His eyes were Caribbean blue, the same shape as Brooks's. Had the same playful sparkle, too. Well, that she remembered, at least.

"Your shop is beautiful," she said. "I saw the sign about lessons…" She waved toward the general direction of the window. "I was just curious."

Leaning against the counter, he steepled his hands in front of his snakeskin belt. "You look familiar to me, darling. Do I know you from somewhere?"

Daisy's stomach dropped. She couldn't believe that he'd recognize her after all these years. He knew so many people—they had to come in and out of his life like locusts. But still, there was no denying the way he was looking at her now, like he was trying his best to place her.

She licked her lips, briefly considering lying. But she hated lying, and she'd told enough whoppers lately to last a lifetime. Besides, Eddie would eventually figure it out anyway. If he hated her for breaking his son's heart, then so be it. She'd take her medicine as gracefully as she could swallow it down.

She smiled, pushing all the memories away where they couldn't hurt her. Brooks had been an important person in her life, but that was years ago. His father was no longer someone she hoped to get to know and someday have a relationship with. To maybe someday be a daughter to. Those were little girl dreams, and she was a woman now. With realistic expectations and things she needed to make right. Even small things, like having a brief, but meaningful conversation about the past. She owed Brooks that. And she owed herself that, too.

"Actually," she said, "I dated your son in high school. I dated Brooks."

She watched as a slow recognition settled on Eddie's face. She felt like a rabbit caught in a snare and braced herself.

He snapped his fingers. "Daisy...right?"

"That's right. I'm surprised you remember."

"Oh, doll. How could I forget? You were the love of Brooks's life."

The impact of that tiny little sentence was like a wave

washing over her, threatening to knock her right off her feet. She felt dizzy, overwhelmed by it all. With Brooks, with making amends with Lily, with coming to terms with her mother's death. Maybe it was just now catching up to her, and she was finally going to have some kind of episode right here in Eddie Cole's new music shop.

He put a hand on her elbow. "Are you okay, darling? You look a bit peaked."

"I'm alright. Just a little tired, I guess."

He watched her, seeming unconvinced.

"You know," she said, "I just wanted to tell you how much Brooks meant to me in high school." She could barely believe she was going there, but she needed to tell him. Or maybe she needed to tell someone, so that she could hear herself say it out loud and reconcile it in her heart. It was time.

"He helped me through a really hard time in my life, and I ended up leaving," she plowed on. "Mostly because I loved him and I couldn't have him, and I just couldn't take that. It wasn't about anything he did. It was about me. And, well…I just wanted you to know. That I loved him."

A slow, tender smile spread across Eddie Cole's mouth. He reached out and patted her arm again, but this time he didn't seem worried he'd need to catch her if she fell.

"He loved you too, doll," Eddie said. "You were both so young. You still had a lot to figure out."

She nodded. Not trusting herself to say any more without crying, which would mortify her beyond belief.

Eddie seemed to sense this and took a deep breath. "So," he said. "About those lessons…"

"Oh, no. I can't. I mean, I would. I just have too much going on right now."

"Too much to set aside thirty minutes a week? At a discount?"

Daisy felt her face color. He was being so sweet. "I can't let you do that."

"Why not? This is why I retired here. To spend some time with people and get to know them again. That includes my sons. And their friends."

"Well, I wouldn't say we're friends anymore. But he might be my boss at some point. I applied for a job out at his ranch."

"Ahh. Well, you will be busy then. We'll just have to work around your schedule."

She looked down at the bag of cookies in her hand, feeling a genuine stirring of excitement. Then looked back up and nodded slowly. "Okay, Mr. Cole. You've got yourself a student."

He opened his mouth to reply, but her phone buzzed from her pocket. She dug it out and looked at the caller ID. It was a Marietta number.

"I'm sorry," she said. "Can I take this really quick?"

"Be my guest."

Daisy made her way over to the front door and answered

the phone with her pulse fluttering behind her ear.

"Hello?"

"You start tomorrow," Brooks said. "Nine sharp. Don't be late."

The phone went dead before she could answer. She stood there staring out the window to the lights on Main Street. It was almost dark now. People were walking by licking ice cream cones and holding shopping bags. Faint stars twinkled in the heavens above, celestial glitter spread across the big, dusky sky.

And she smiled.

Chapter Five

Sharpen your knives!

BROOKS WATCHED THE old Jeep making its way up the drive. He leaned against the porch railing and grunted when Porter walked by and punched him in the arm.

"It'll be fine," Porter said. "She'll do a great job."

"Yeah. Well. I'll blame you when she doesn't."

He glared at his brother's retreating form. Sure, Porter thought it was going to be great. Everyone thought it was going to be great. Even Charlie was excited about their new hire and had promised to come out today to start showing her the ropes.

Brooks, on the other hand, couldn't get his mind wrapped around the fact that he'd actually pulled the trigger on this. It had been a weak moment. Or something like that, and now he'd have to live with the consequences. Which, he had no doubt, would be significant.

The Jeep slowed as it neared the house, then came to a stop, the cloud of dust behind it settling in the bright morning sunlight. Birds sang cheerfully in the leafy maples next to the porch, completely unaware of Brooks's sour mood.

He watched as Daisy opened the passenger door and climbed out, her skirt riding briefly over her smooth thighs.

Lily waved through the open window at Brooks, and he waved back. He'd always liked Lily. She and Daisy had it rough growing up and had been close. He had to admit it was nice seeing them together again. He loved his brothers and didn't know what he would've done without them over the years. He was glad Lily had her sister back.

Daisy hauled out a big, purple suitcase from the back of the Jeep and stood clutching it as Lily pulled slowly out of the gravel drive.

She looked up at him and smiled. "Most of my things are still in storage. I figured this is all I'll need for now, anyway."

Not bothering to smile back, he took the porch steps two by two.

"Here. I can take that."

"Thank you."

She handed the suitcase over and tugged her fitted tank top down over her waist. It had inched up, exposing a sliver of belly, and his gaze dropped there before he could help it.

"I'll show you your room," he said gruffly.

He heard her footsteps behind him, short and quick, where his were long and purposeful. She was nervous, and he was being an ass. But he couldn't help it. Or maybe he didn't want to help it, which was different. He felt a momentary pang of guilt, before he shoved it away again. He'd hired her. He figured that was showing enough grace to last him a while.

Holding the suitcase in one hand, he pulled the screen door open and waited as she brushed past. She smelled like vanilla, something else that he pushed aside. He didn't need to be noticing how she smelled. Or how she looked, with her long blond hair falling in silky waves past her shoulders. He didn't need to be noticing anything about her, except how well she did her job. That was it.

He walked in after her and let the screen door slam behind him. The house was quiet this morning. Too quiet. They were between guests, and Porter had disappeared— probably heading out to feed the horses at the most infuriating time. At the moment, it was just him and Daisy, and the entire house seemed to be holding its breath.

"Your room is right up here," he said, heading toward the staircase. She followed him up, her strappy sandals tapping on the hardwood. "It's pretty small, but I went out and got a few things to make it a little more homey."

His neck heated. He hadn't needed to mention that. The fact that he'd gone into town last night and bought some sheer white curtains for her window that faced the river in the distance. And a couple of throw pillows with little flowers all over them that had reminded him of his aunt's garden growing up. Daisy had always liked that garden.

Coming to the room at the end of the hallway now, he

pushed open the door and set her suitcase down by the closet. "Here you go," he said.

She stepped over to the window and parted the curtains. Then turned around to look at the rest of the room. Her eyes were bright.

"It's just perfect, Brooks," she said quietly. "Thank you."

"It's nothing. Just a room."

She watched him.

"You can just…" He cleared his throat. "Unpack, or whatever. And then when you're ready, you can come down and I'll show you where everything is…"

He let his voice trail off, feeling awkward and kind of like a bull in a damn china shop around her. He turned to go, telling himself that he didn't care anyway.

"Brooks?"

He looked over. Her brown eyes were glassy now, and she was biting her cheek. He remembered she used to do that to keep from crying. She'd cried a lot as a girl.

"Thank you," she said. "Not just for the room. But for the job. For giving me a chance."

She was standing in a morning sunbeam. It slanted through the window, bathing her in gold. Tiny dust particles floated all around her, reminding him of stars. She was so pretty, that for a second, his heart couldn't take it. For a second, he couldn't imagine what on earth had possessed Alex to let her go. He must've been out of his mind. But then, she'd been Brooks's too once, hadn't she? Once upon a time. So he was in no position to judge.

"You're welcome," he said.

They stood there for a long minute, looking at each other. And then Elvira sauntered in with a meow. She sniffed the suitcase, decided it could stay, then hopped up on the bed, and began cleaning herself with her sandpaper tongue.

"Nope," Brooks said. "Don't think so."

"She can stay. It's alright."

He looked over at Daisy, ready to argue. Elvira had her run of the place, but they kept her out of the bedrooms as a general rule. People who were allergic to cats didn't appreciate her stray hairs that had a tendency to float through the air and never land.

"Please?" she said. "I'd actually love the company."

He grit his teeth. He couldn't argue with that. And he couldn't say no to those big, dark eyes, which would end up being a problem if he let it.

"Alright. But if you get sick of her, just put her out in the hallway. She's got a bed out there."

"I won't get sick of her." Daisy leaned over and scratched the cat behind her ears. It was like she'd pulled a lawn mower cord. You could hear the purr a mile away.

"She's fairly spoiled."

Daisy laughed. "She just knows what she wants. Can't blame a girl for that."

"Mostly she just wants bacon. She won't leave you alone when you're cooking. Fair warning."

"Got it."

"Porter might be a problem, too. He'll come in there and talk your ear off."

"I don't mind." She looked up at him. "What about you?"

"What about me?"

"Do you like to hang out in the kitchen, too?"

"I'll stay out of your way. Unless you're making something where I can lick the bowl."

He smiled. Then remembered he wasn't supposed to like her anymore and looked away. "I'll just get out of your hair," he said evenly. "Meet me downstairs when you're ready."

DAISY WALKED ALONG the drive leading back to the ranch house and pulled her sweater tighter around her shoulders. A full moon was just peeking its mottled, silver head over Copper Mountain in the distance, and a chorus of full-throated frogs croaked in the surrounding pastures. Somewhere to her left, doves cooed to each other, a bedtime story that was as soft and sweet as the summer evening itself. But as beautiful as it was, as lovely as the ranch looked in the newborn moonlight, she still felt a little sad.

Looking over at the barn, she listened to her ballet flats crunch along the gravel and thought of Boston in the evenings—the city twinkling like the Milky Way, the sounds of sirens and people and life, even in the latest hours of the night, or the earliest hours of the morning when the world should still be sleeping. She'd been alone many, many nights in Boston, but she'd never really felt lonely. She'd had a few close girlfriends. And she'd had her work at Saint Nicholas. It had been challenging, which had given her a quiet confidence and strength that had kept her afloat all these years.

Here, at the ranch, she was a fish out of water. It was humbling and scary. She'd talked herself into a job that she wasn't realistically sure she could manage, at least not very well.

She pulled in a deep breath and filled her lungs with the sweet air of the countryside—of animals and grass, and wildflowers that grew along the wide, bumpy lane. So different than Boston, which smelled like hot cement and taxi exhaust.

Wrapping her arms around herself, Daisy stopped and watched as a tall, shadowy figure led a horse into one of the turnouts and let it go with a light slap on the rump. Her heart thumped behind her breastbone as she recognized the familiar tilt of the man's head, the way his lean body moved in the moonlight. Besides Lily, Brooks was the only one she'd ever allowed past her walls as a kid. When she and her mother had fought, when she'd been hurting the most, Brooks had always been there. And when he hadn't wanted to get married after high school? Well, all she could think about was her own father not wanting to settle down. And look where that had left her mom. Alone and bitter and heartbroken.

Daisy had been so determined that she wasn't going to end up alone, that she'd married the wrong man, just so she could fall asleep to the comforting sounds of him breathing next to her. How screwed up was that?

Very.

She watched Brooks walk out of the turnout and close the gate behind him. She stepped up to the pasture fence and rested her hands there, the splintered wood poking into the soft flesh of her fingertips. She was pretty sure he couldn't see her in the darkness, but she didn't want to take any chances. He might feel the need to come over and say hello, and she was feeling so out of sorts, she didn't trust herself with that. Or with him, for that matter. Tonight, it was hard to tell if she was still in love with Brooks, or if she was still in love with the thought of him. That happily ever after that she'd always longed for, but had never found.

He walked toward the house, his broad shoulders hunched a little. She knew he was still mad at her. Of course he was. But he'd been incredibly kind in giving her this job, anyway. She hoped she wouldn't screw it up. Tomorrow morning she'd cook her first dude ranch breakfast. There were no guests to feed at the moment, so for a dry run it would be pretty safe. But in a few days, a large group was coming in from Oregon, and they'd expect meals that didn't taste like charcoal.

She pushed off the fence and smiled as Brooks was met by Clifford on the porch steps. The little dog wiggled at his feet before they headed inside, the soft, yellow lights winking on in the living room windows.

Daisy tilted her head back and looked up at the moon. It was a beautiful glowing orb in the night sky, bathing the world below in its magic dust. A moon only Montana could conjure. She missed Boston. But she didn't think any place on earth could offer up a moon as pretty as this one.

And right then, she chose to accept it with the proper amount of gratitude in her heart.

"Thank you," she whispered. To nobody in particular.

Chapter Six

Cook them low and slow...

DAISY STOOD IN the lovely old kitchen wearing her mother's red apron, a last-minute gift from Lily to go with the cookbook. She'd pulled her hair back in a ponytail, which had been a smart choice, since the morning was already warm. She'd opened the windows to let the breeze in, but she'd also wanted fresh air circulating just in case she burned something right off the bat.

She looked down at the cookbook, which was open to *Breakfasts*, and ran her fingertips along her mother's familiar, slanty writing. *Beat eggs, milk, salt and pepper in medium bowl until well blended...* She could almost hear her mom saying this. With one hand on her hip, and the other on her favorite yellow mixing bowl.

Daisy's heart squeezed as she remembered her mother in the kitchen. Her happy place. The place where she'd probably felt the most in control of her young life. By the time Lou Hudson was thirty-five, she was a single mother of two teenage girls whose father had taken off before they'd even had a chance to know him. She'd gone prematurely gray, her once sunny smile turning hard and cool. Daisy could barely remember her mother's smile. But she could remember her in the kitchen, working over her stove and looking as close to content as she probably ever was.

Daisy reached for the bowl of eggs across the counter. Her mom's scrambled eggs had been the best in three counties. She'd told her oldest daughter once that the secret to great cooking was quality ingredients. *Try and use farm-fresh eggs when you can,* she'd said. *Remember that.* And then she'd tweaked her nose. A rare and coveted show of affection.

Daisy grazed her bottom lip with her teeth. Despite everything, her mother would be proud of her this morning. There was no doubt about that. Not only was she cooking with her cookbook, but she was using the freshest eggs possible. She'd gone out to the hen house at dawn and gathered them herself. She felt like a certified pioneer woman trudging back to the house, the eggs still warm against her belly.

The screen door slammed now, startling her from her thoughts. She glanced up at the clock above the stove. She'd told Porter and Brooks that breakfast would be ready by nine. After they fed the horses and cattle, but before their morning chores. She was already running behind and felt a tickle of nerves in her lower belly.

"Morning."

She turned toward the sound of the gravelly voice behind

her. But she already knew who it was. She'd known the second she'd heard his boots clomp across the living room floor—a familiar, steady cadence that seemed to keep time with the beat of her heart.

Brooks stood there in the archway of the kitchen. He held his black Stetson in one hand, his hair damp with sweat. His neck glistened with it, and Daisy had to work not to stare. After all these years, he could still affect her like he had when she was seventeen.

"Good morning," she said, smoothing her apron. "I hope you're hungry. I'm making extra bacon."

He smiled, two long dimples cutting into his stubbly cheeks. "You can never go wrong with extra bacon."

He hadn't given her too many genuine smiles since she'd gotten here, but that was definitely one for the books. *Bacon.* She'd have to remember that.

She looked down at Elvira who'd appeared like an apparition and was rubbing herself against his boots. Charmed, no doubt, by whatever he'd recently stepped in.

"I think she heard the magic word," she said.

"I told you, she's gonna be a pest. You might want to toss her outside while you're cooking."

"Oh, that's okay. I need a taste tester anyway."

She reached over to turn on the stove, where a shiny pan sat waiting and ever-hopeful.

Brooks ran a hand through his hair. "Okay, then…I'll just get cleaned up."

Daisy nodded, thinking that he looked just fine without getting cleaned up. In fact, she could get used to the sweat and how it complimented his bronzed skin and ropy muscles. Which worried her. Brooks was her boss now. And noticing how his sweat complimented anything, was not in her job description.

He turned to leave, and her gaze dropped to his Wrangler-clad buns. Her cheeks heated. *Definitely* not in her job description.

She forced her attention back to the open package of bacon on the counter. Taking a breath, she got several slices out, and lay them on the pan where they began a satisfying, country sizzle. She adjusted the heat a little, before picking up the whisk and bowl to beat the eggs. *So far, so good...*

Elvira meowed at her feet, blinking up at her with an expectant look.

"I'll save you some. Promise."

The cat meowed again and wrapped herself around Daisy's ankles, her fur like silk against her skin. She could see how this could be dangerous. Cute, but definitely a tripping hazard.

Holding the mixing bowl against her hip, she checked the bacon to make sure it wasn't burning and gave the cat a gentle nudge with her foot. She was officially multitasking. Which could end up being good. Or not so good... "I hear you, honey. I'd want bacon too if I had to eat cat food every day."

Elvira mewed in agreement.

"But you're going to make me break my face on my first day, and then we'll both be in a heap of trouble."

Meeeoooowww.

Daisy laughed and turned her attention back to the bowl. "Goodness. I get it. Believe me."

She whipped the eggs, listening to the comforting sound of the bacon frying in the pan, of the whisk tapping against the sides of the bowl, of water running from the faucet in the next room over. Brooks cleaning up. She tried not to picture what that would look like, but it was a losing battle. Before she could help it, she imagined his plaid shirt slung over the bathroom door, his jeans riding low on his narrow hips. Tap water beading over his neck and chest, before he grabbed a towel to rub himself dry.

Her blood warmed in her veins. It didn't help that she knew exactly what Brooks looked like without a shirt on. Yes, he'd changed since high school. But as far as she could tell, those changes only enhanced what he'd had going on before. And what he had going on before, was plenty.

She focused on the eggs in the bowl and began humming her favorite Luke Combs song as a distraction. If she was going to survive this job, she'd need to get her head on straight. She was a little lonesome, yes. And seeing Brooks again was bringing back feelings that she thought she'd safely buried. That was true, too. But she'd come home again to start fresh, and that didn't include lusting after her old boyfriend who'd said no when she'd asked him to marry her. The rejection, the pain inflicted by that tiny little word, had shaped the direction of her entire life.

Sprinkling some salt and pepper into the bowl, she felt the sting of that memory now almost as sharply as she'd felt it then. Because if Brooks, her one true love, wasn't going to make her happy, then who was?

She knew the answer to that question now. But it had taken a long time to figure it out, a lot of soul searching and looking back, in order to be able to look forward once and for all. She was going to have to make herself happy. She would never allow anyone else to be the source of her joy again. But that didn't mean it would be easy. It was going to be hard as hell.

Behind her, there was another insistent mew, but she didn't turn around. If she didn't give this breakfast her full attention, it might not turn out to be edible, and that was her *only* job description.

"If you can wait a few minutes," she said over her shoulder, "I'll pour some bacon fat over your food. How does that sound?"

The cat didn't respond. Probably sick of asking.

Daisy smiled. Then turned to look down at her. "I—"

Only she wasn't sitting on the sunny patch of linoleum where she'd been before. That particular spot was empty, sans cat. Instead, something black caught the corner of Daisy's eye, and she looked up to see Elvira on the counter.

Right next to the pan of bacon.

Daisy sucked in a breath as Elvira touched the handle with her paw. "*No!*" she whisper-yelled.

But before she could take a step toward her, the cat pushed. It was a little push. A curious push. The kind of push that would scoot an empty water bottle off the edge of a coffee table. Or the kind that would unseat a pan of bacon unwisely sitting on the front burner of the stove. *Use the back burner if you can*, she heard her mother saying in her ear. A cooking tip that she'd forgotten until this very moment, and one she'd probably never forget again.

Elvira was nonplussed. She gave the pan another little shove. Her paw caught the handle just right to make it slide across the glass cooktop like an ice skater over Miracle Lake. Easy-peasy. On a trajectory straight to the floor.

Daisy gasped, able to see how it would all unfold a second from now—partially cooked bacon strips laying limp across the linoleum, hot grease dripping from cabinets. Evidence of a breakfast murder scene. Her first attempt at a dude ranch meal, a case for a really bored CSI team.

Without thinking, she reached for the pan before it teetered over the edge. Only wanting to save the bacon. And her pride. That was on the line, too.

She meant to grab the handle but overshot. Before her brain could tell her hand to pull back, her fingers connected with the side of the hot pan, stopping it before it tumbled to the floor.

"Ouch!"

Elvira bolted at the sound of her voice, sending a pot-holder and a few stray recipe cards flying.

Holding her hand against her chest, Daisy pushed the bacon off the heat. She might've burned all her fingerprints off, but at least she'd saved breakfast. And if she ever wanted to rob a bank in the future, she was good to go.

"What happened?"

She squeezed her eyes shut at the sound of the voice behind her. *Crap.* She'd really wanted today to go smoothly. She'd wanted to make a hearty meal for two hungry cowboys and earn a paycheck through sheer grit and determination. True, the bacon hadn't gone all over the floor. But injuring herself on the job in the first ten minutes wasn't exactly how she'd define smooth.

Forcing a smile, she turned, moving her hand behind her back. And then her heartbeat slowed. Brooks was standing there, dripping wet and clutching a towel loosely around his waist. Her fantasy from a few minutes ago, bigger than life and in glorious Technicolor right before her eyes. Water dripped from his slicked-back hair, jet-black in the morning light. It ran seductively down his neck, beading on his defined chest. Unlike when he was a teenager, there was a scattering of dark hair there now, just enough to make a woman want to run her fingers over it and feel its coarseness underneath her hands.

She knew she was staring. She knew it, but she couldn't

seem to remember what she'd been about to say. Or what he'd said to require a response in the first place.

She cleared her throat, struggling for her bearings. Or at least some of them, which would do in a pinch. "Uh…nothing."

He narrowed his eyes. "Why are you standing like that?"

"Like what?"

"Like that. Like you're hiding something behind your back."

"No reason. It's just how I stand." She smiled wider, feeling ridiculous. Of course he knew she was hiding something. But she couldn't seem to come clean just yet. Maybe it was pure old-fashioned stubbornness. Or maybe, she was just enjoying the current view too much. It was a good one.

Scowling, he stepped forward, the towel slipping just enough that she caught a glimpse of muscled thigh.

Brooks glanced over at the bacon, cooling in the pan. Then at the recipe cards scattered over the floor. Then back at Daisy, his hazel eyes sharp. "Let me see your hand."

She shook her head. "I'm fine."

"I didn't ask how you were."

"Brooks, no. Go away."

"You can't tell me to go away. I'm your boss, remember?"

He had a point. One she'd forgotten in the heat of the moment.

Jaw twitching, he reached around her. Then found her

wrist and encircled it in his hand. It was like a steel trap. Brooks had always had big hands, even as a boy. Big, strong, capable hands, with veins snaking over his long, blocky fingers. She'd always loved his hands.

She gasped at the boldness of it. He smelled like soap and shampoo, his skin warm and damp against hers. She hadn't been this close to him in over a decade, but her body remembered exactly how to feel, what to do. Her back arched reflexively, her breasts jutting toward him in an instinctive effort to get closer. She checked herself immediately, but it was too late. He must've noticed.

His gaze locked with hers, and she raised her chin, hoping to regain some dignity. She no longer cared about the pulsing pain in her fingertips. The ache in her heart was much, much worse.

Still clutching his towel, he pulled her hand out from behind her back and looked down at it. Not wanting to, Daisy looked down at it, too. Her fingertips were red and already blistering. It wasn't a terrible burn, as far as burns went, but it was bad enough, and all of a sudden her knees felt weak. She swayed a little.

"Whoa." Brooks touched her shoulder and held her steady. "You okay?"

"Fine. Just woozy. It's probably the heat."

"It's probably the fact that you just burned yourself, and burns hurt like hell."

It might also have to do with the fact that he was now

standing so close that her breasts were rubbing against his chest in his effort to keep her upright. What she really wanted to do was sag against him. Let him carry her straight to the couch and set her down, and touch her face like he used to. He'd had a way of brushing her hair back that had made her feel like a movie star.

Instead, she forced a deep breath and locked her knees in place.

"Come here." Still holding her hand, he led her over to the dining room table and pulled out a chair. "Sit."

She lowered herself down while carefully avoiding the view of his half-naked body right in front of her face.

Once she was seated, he headed over to the cabinet by the microwave, dug around in a small box, and pulled out of tube of ointment.

He came back over and sank to one knee. "Give me your hand."

She let him take it, looking down at the top of his wet head, and wanting to touch his hair. Wanting to put her lips against it and breathe in the smell of his shampoo.

He squeezed some ointment out of the tube and dabbed it on the tip of her fingers. The pain was immediate and pulsing, and she winced.

"I'm sorry," he said, looking up at her. "Does that hurt?"

She nodded, in danger of getting lost in those eyes. She thought that when she took this job, she could handle being near Brooks again. And she could. At least, she thought she could. But being near him, and having him touch her, take care of her, were two very different things. Especially when he wasn't dressed. She wondered if he was experiencing any of this in the least. Probably not. Her faded red apron was far from sexy, and her hair was clinging in damp tendrils to the back of her neck. The idea of having the windows open for the fresh, summer air had been romantic, but not really practical. It was too warm in the kitchen to be comfortable, and all of a sudden, she felt deflated. And defeated.

She stared down at him, her heart beating steadily against her rib cage. He was studying her hand, in deep concentration as he worked the ointment over the blisters. She swallowed hard, her tongue feeling thick and dry in her mouth.

"Do you ever think about us?" she asked.

The words were out and hanging between them before she could even process what she'd said.

His fingers stopped moving over hers. He held her hand still and looked up.

"I'm sorry?"

She shook her head. "Nothing."

From outside the open windows, there was the cheerful whinny of a horse, the muted sound of a truck rumbling by on the highway. Birds, chirping at the feeder on the porch. But the kitchen was suddenly quiet. Waiting for him to say something. Anything.

He took a breath, then let it out again, and placed her

hand back on her lap.

"If you're asking if I ever think about us like that," he said, "the answer is no."

She watched him, hurt by that. Knowing full well she had no right. She'd been the one to leave, after all. But even when she'd thought she'd put Brooks behind her, she knew now that she hadn't. Deep down, he'd always been there. It wasn't so much that she wanted to be with him again, as she wanted him to be happy. So really, the fact that he'd moved on was good. She was doing her best to move on, too.

She smiled. "I have no idea why I asked you that," she said. "It was awkward. Sorry."

He looked away for a few seconds. When he looked back, there was more color in his handsome face than before.

"It was hard getting over you, Daisy," he said, his voice low. "I worked at it for a long time, but I finally got right again. I'm good now. We're good now, right?"

She nodded again, her throat aching. "Of course. Of course we are."

He still hadn't taken his hand off her thigh. She was hyper-aware of its weight, of its warmth. He moved his thumb in a small arc, and the slight motion made her toes curl. Were they good? She guessed they would be if he didn't touch her anymore.

"I guess I feel like we need to talk about it at some point," she said. "To clear the air."

"Nothing to clear."

"Okay. But I just want you to know…it's important to me that you know, it was hard getting over you, too."

His mouth settled into a hard line.

"I know I was the one to leave, Brooks," she said. "But I left because you didn't want me."

"Excuse me?"

"You didn't. I remember that pretty clearly."

"You're not remembering right, then."

She should've left it alone. But she'd been right in thinking they needed to clear the air. It was all there, still bubbling underneath the surface. How were they ever going to have a decent working relationship with it festering like this? And yeah, maybe it wasn't as much of an issue for him, but it definitely was for her.

"That day on the dock?" she bit out. "I wanted to marry you. And you said no. That you didn't want to settle down."

"I didn't."

"Well, there you have it."

"I didn't want to settle down traditionally, but I damn sure didn't want to break up. My issue with marriage didn't have anything to do with you."

She laughed. "How could it not? You knew how I felt about making a commitment to each other."

His face was getting red. A couple of small veins stood out on his temple. She didn't care. She was mad, too. This morning was really going to hell in a handbasket.

She pushed his hand off her thigh. "Thank you for the

ointment. But I should get back to work." She tried to stand, but he held her arm.

"Now wait," he said. "Wait just a damn minute. You don't get to be pissed here."

"And why not?"

"Because you're the one who ran off with my best friend, remember?"

"Because we broke *up*, Brooks."

"We broke up because you refused to see anything my way. You refused to see anything anyone's way, except your own. Stubborn, headstrong, pain in my ass…"

Her ears burned. "You were right. I never should've tried talking this out."

"Exactly."

"I just wanted us to start fresh. Is that so bad?"

"It is when we just end up right back where we left off."

"Okay. So we'll agree to leave it alone then."

He scowled up at her, still crouching in his towel. Still dripping and muscular and marvelous. "Agreed."

She scowled back. She felt ten times worse than before, if that was even possible. She felt upside down, inside out. Even turned on, God help her. And what she really wanted to do was storm out, but she had a breakfast to cook, and she absolutely couldn't burn it. She didn't have the luxury of melting down like a teenager.

"Um, is this a new dress code I'm not aware of?"

They both looked up to see Porter standing in the archway. Smiling like a juvenile delinquent.

Brooks shot him a look. "Shut up."

"Whoa."

"I just burned my hand," Daisy said. "And Brooks was putting some ointment on it."

"Naked," Porter said, taking his hat off. He was clearly enjoying himself.

"I'm not naked, asshole. I've got a towel on."

"Oh, well then. A *towel*."

Daisy felt herself flush all the way to her scalp.

"What are you guys talking about?" Porter asked, leaning casually against the fridge.

"None of your business," Brooks said.

Daisy smiled self-consciously, feeling like they'd just been caught having a lover's quarrel, which was ridiculous, since they weren't lovers anymore. And they also apparently hated each other. "Nothing. Just clearing the air."

"Oh?"

"Get lost, Porter." This from Brooks, who stood, holding the towel firmly around his waist.

"Last I checked, this was my kitchen too, towel boy. And isn't it breakfast time?"

"It is," Daisy said, standing, too.

She accidentally brushed Brooks's bare arm in the process, and he jerked away, putting some distance between them. She glared at him. What did he think she was going to do? Jump his bones right here in the kitchen? She wasn't that desperate.

Porter was taking it all in, looking from one of them, to the other. He and Brooks were twins, but the only thing they had in common was their good looks. Right now, they couldn't have appeared more different—Porter mischievous and teasing, and Brooks brooding and dark.

Elvira strolled in and gazed up at them. As if she had no idea why breakfast wasn't ready yet.

Daisy gave her a wary look. "I'll just get back to it," she said, straightening her apron.

"I'll get you some Band-Aids," Brooks said.

"I'm fine."

"I'll go get dressed then."

Porter smirked at him as he stalked past. After a second, the bedroom door slammed.

"What the hell was that all about?" Porter asked.

"Same old fight. We still don't understand each other."

"What's to understand? You were crazy about each other. You're probably still crazy about each other."

Daisy bent to pick up the recipe cards from the floor. "I wouldn't necessarily say that."

"Really? I think it's pretty obvious."

"He hates me."

"He's pissed at you. There's a difference."

"I never should've left Marietta," she said, standing, and tucking the recipe cards back into the elderly cookbook. "I never should've left Brooks, at least not like that. I shouldn't have left my family. Who does that?"

Porter put his hat back on, then stepped toward her with his hands in his pockets. He smelled like ranch, like sweat and hard work. Daisy was only now seeing how much it took to run this place. And there weren't even guests here at the moment. She had no idea how they made time to sleep.

"You need to start giving yourself a break," Porter said. "You had it rough."

She smiled slightly and touched the cookbook cover with her burned fingertips. It hurt to touch it. It hurt to look at it. Despite everything, despite that rough upbringing, she missed her mother right then, so much she didn't think she could take it.

"Lots of people have hard childhoods," she said. "You and Brooks and Griffin had it hard. At least in the beginning."

"Yeah. But we always knew we were loved. I mean, basically. You couldn't ever say that."

No, she couldn't. At least not with any certainty. Lou Hudson could be frigid when she wanted to be. It was only now that she was gone that Daisy was starting to see she'd probably used that side of her personality to keep people out. If she never let them in, how much damage could they really do? Even her own daughters had been casualties of that emotional armor.

Daisy looked up at Porter. "Thank you for being so sweet. It's going to take a while to process all of this. Being home again. But I'll get there."

"Brooks will get there, too. Don't worry."

And what would happen when he did? Would they settle into a healthy professional relationship? Or would they be able to take it one step further and actually be friends?

Daisy hoped they'd be friends. She'd missed him too much to be happy with anything less.

Chapter Seven

Practice makes perfect!

"**L**IKE THIS? I can't get this thing to cooperate."

Brooks walked across the dusty arena, toward the middle-aged man in glasses and khakis. Sure enough, the lasso was tangled around his feet like a snake getting ready to eat something.

He gave the guy a hearty slap on the back. His name was Owen. Brooks liked him. He was trying, and he wasn't afraid of getting dirty. Even though he was wearing the same damn clothes he probably wore to the office every day.

Owen and his self-professed computer geek coworkers were here from Portland, Oregon, on a three-week summer retreat meant to build teamwork and camaraderie. Apparently, the owner, an eccentric millennial with deep pockets, had a penchant for offering his employees these kinds of adventures. Owen said working for this tech company was like being at summer camp half the year. So far, it seemed like they were all having fun. But it was only day three, so who could tell. Brooks had seen these types of things go south pretty fast. First time someone got stepped on by a cow, or lost their glasses on a trail ride, even the most cheerful camaraderie had a tendency to deteriorate.

Brooks bent down to pick up the rope. Then threw most of it back down in the dirt, keeping hold of the tail.

"You're doing great," he said. "But you can't get ahead of yourself. One of the first things you need to learn is how to coil this bad boy." He held the rope out an arm's length. "Just hold it like this, flip it over to where it's laying right, then bring it back in to where it makes a nice circle. Then keep doing that until you've got an even coil."

Owen sighed. "You make it look easy. I've been messing with it for ten minutes and can't get it to look like that."

"If you did it all day every day, you'd make it look easy, too. Believe me, it's just repetition and practice. Ready to build your loop?"

Owen nodded. He was sporting a new sunburn across his nose, and looked healthier, more energized than when he'd arrived a few days ago. Maybe he was a Pacific Northwest cowboy in the making. "Ready as I'll ever be," he said.

"Alright then. You hold it right here. By the hondo, where the rope is running through itself. You just slide it through like this, until you build the loop. See?"

"I think so. Maybe."

"By Friday, you'll be throwing like a pro."

Owen looked skeptically around at his coworkers, some of whom were tossing their lassos in the general direction of the roping dummies in the middle of the arena. His gaze settled on a short, plump man, who was untangling himself from his lasso, and sweating profusely through his polo. Brooks really needed to go over appropriate ranching attire again. The guy had passed an acceptable amount of sun an hour ago and was now working his way toward lobsterville.

"As long as I rope something before Romano," Owen mumbled. "I can't stand that guy."

"Oh yeah?"

"He's a blowhard."

"Well, that's why you're here, remember? To get to know each other? Maybe he's not as bad as you think."

Owen pushed his glasses up. "No amount of dude ranching and soul searching is going to get me to tolerate Romano. But I appreciate the effort, though."

Brooks laughed. "Fair enough." He held the rope steady, then began swinging the lasso over his head.

"You look like Clint Eastwood," Owen said dryly. "Legitimately."

"Practice. It's all in the wrist. See how I'm pointing my finger down the shaft? Pointing it right at the calf."

Owen watched as Brooks let the rope fly. The lasso arced through the air, briefly standing out against the cobalt Montana sky, before landing with a *thwack* around the dummy.

Brooks yanked the rope tight. "See? Easy, once you get the hang of it."

Owen wasn't listening. He was now gazing toward the house.

Brooks looked over, too. There, walking toward them, was Daisy. She was balancing a tray of drinks and had a small cooler slung over one bronzed shoulder. Her white sundress flared out from her hips, and her hair tumbled in silky, honey-colored ripples down her back.

"Wow," Owen said under his breath. Brooks couldn't blame him. In fact, most of the men in the group had stopped messing with their lassos and were gazing over at the woman walking through the open gate now. Although, at this point it was hard to tell what was turning them on more—the sight of Daisy, or the sight of the cold drinks on her tray. Brooks could almost make out the icy condensation from where he stood.

He took his Stetson off and wiped his forehead with the back of his hand. What he was thinking, but obviously couldn't say, was that he knew exactly what she looked like *out* of that dress, and wow wasn't a strong enough word.

Daisy set the drinks down on a picnic table by the fence, then took the cooler strap off her shoulder, and set that down, too.

"Who's hungry?" she asked.

There was an eager murmur throughout the group, as she opened up the cooler and began handing out sandwiches with the lemonade.

She looked over at Brooks and smiled. He had to admit,

she was killing this part. She had settled into hostess mode effortlessly and was perfect with the guests. They loved her, and she seemed to love them right back. In the last few days, he'd noticed her chatting them up—asking where they were from, what they did for a living, asking about their families. She seemed to have a way of making them feel special, which couldn't be taught. Brooks and Porter had had several employees over the years, and either they had the knack, or they didn't. Daisy had it. And then some.

Owen came back with a juicy turkey sandwich on white bread and took a big bite.

"Oh mer good," he mumbled, his mouth full. "I'm so herngry."

When everyone had a sandwich and had settled in the shade of the big willow to eat, Daisy made her way over, too. She brushed her hands down her dress, smoothing it, before bestowing a bewitching smile on Owen.

"I don't think we've officially met," she said, extending a slender hand. "I'm Daisy Hudson."

Owen smiled back and shook it. "Owen Douglas. Pleased to meet you."

"I hope you're having a nice time, Owen. We're so happy to have you."

"I've never been to Montana before. I can't believe how beautiful it is."

"Have you gone into Marietta yet?" Daisy asked. "Cutest little shops. Nice restaurants. If you like Italian, Rocco's is my favorite."

Brooks watched her. They'd had their first kiss at Rocco's. Homecoming, sophomore year. He still remembered her dress—blue, with tiny white polka dots.

"I *love* Italian." Owen patted his belly.

"Well, if you go, leave room for chocolate after," Daisy said. "Copper Mountain Chocolate Shop is the best around. And Sage has gift boxes if you want to bring some home."

"Good to know." Owen took another bite of his sandwich, then washed it down with a gulp of lemonade. "Hey, question…"

"Yeah." Brooks and Daisy answered in unison and looked at each other.

Owen noticed and grinned. "Do you do much fishing out of that river?"

Brooks rubbed the back of his neck. Another memory, sweet and warm, crowded its way to the front of his mind. Fishing with Daisy, the sun hot on their shoulders, the riverbank grass cool in between their toes. They'd done a lot of fishing back then. Fishing and swimming and lying underneath the stars. Counting them one by one, watching the shooting kind burn themselves out against the inkiness of the sky.

"Yeah," Brooks said. "We do a lot of fishing from it. Rainbow trout, mostly. Why? You want to fish?"

Owen shook his head. "No, but I was hoping you'd say trout. Fish is my favorite meal. It was my mom's specialty growing up. She made it with lots of lemon juice and butter, and it was just...well. It was pretty good."

"My mom liked to cook it, too," Daisy said, looking over at Brooks.

He knew her mom had cooked it a lot, because Daisy had brought it home a lot. Probably too many fish to clean some days, truthfully.

Brooks put his hands in his pockets and rocked back on his boots. "You want trout tomorrow night? We could probably make that happen."

Owen lit up. "Seriously? I don't want to put you out."

"We're here to make you happy. If you want trout, trout it is."

"Wow. Then, yes. I'd love that."

Brooks eyed Daisy. "We don't buy our fish at Monroe's. We catch our own here."

She watched him, smiling. Clearly not anticipating where he was going with this.

"Charlie always comes with me," he continued. "Two poles in the water is better than one."

Her smile faded as it began sinking in.

"And you're the new Charlie." He grinned at her, enjoying this more than he probably should be. "Be ready at five."

Chapter Eight

Cook your fish the day you catch them. Or buy them.

DAISY STOOD LOOKING at her reflection in the antique mirror. The light in her bedroom was grainy, the morning sky outside the window just beginning to lighten in the east. She hadn't been up at five in years. Technically, she wasn't a morning person. But she was beginning to see that on a working ranch, there was no other kind of person to be. Coffee was going to be her new best friend.

She blinked at herself and poked at the puffy bags underneath her eyes. She hadn't bothered to shower, opting instead to wash her face and spritz on a light body spray that smelled like lilacs. She'd put her hair back in a ponytail and had pulled it through one of Brooks's baseball caps that he'd let her borrow.

Overall, she thought she looked okay. Not great, but okay. Of course, the fish wouldn't care how she looked. But Brooks might notice, and that had been enough to make her dab on a little lip gloss at the last minute.

Taking a deep breath, she grabbed her small, cross-body

purse, slung it over her hoodie, and reached for the door.

The house was quiet. The guests were either fast asleep or enjoying the early morning solitude in the privacy of their rooms.

She tiptoed down the hallway, knowing by now where the creaky spots were, and made her way down the stairs.

Outside, she could see Brooks's big black truck idling in front of the house.

Butterflies bumped around in her belly as she stopped by the door to pull her boots on. It was just a fishing trip. A fishing trip that Charlie would've gone on herself if she'd been working today instead of Daisy. So it was no big deal. All part of the job...

Except, as she straightened and reached for the door, it did feel like a big deal. Since it was on just this kind of outing where she and Brooks had fallen in love in the first place.

She walked down the steps and toward the truck wearing her most confident smile. The one that said, *friends. Boss. Professional relationship!*

"Good morning," she said, pulling open the truck's heavy passenger side door and climbing in.

He wasn't wearing his cowboy hat this morning, and it was one of the few times she'd seen him without it since coming to work at Diamond in the Rough. Instead, he wore an old trucker hat and a gray hooded sweatshirt. His dark stubble crept down his neck, promising the beginnings of a great beard if he ever decided to grow one.

She yanked the seat belt across her chest.

"How'd you sleep?" he asked, putting the truck into gear and pulling out.

"Great. I mean, I tossed and turned a little because I was worried I'd oversleep. But other than that, great."

He nodded. "I know it's early…"

"That's okay. I love fishing. Or, at least I used to."

"I remember."

They drove toward the highway, the truck bouncing over the ruts in the gravel road. Daisy watched the cattle grazing outside her window and wondered if that's what they did all night long. Did they even sleep? They had to, of course. But did they sleep standing up? What she didn't know about cattle was a lot.

She glanced over at Brooks. "I thought we'd just be walking this morning. To that spot next to the pasture."

"They've been biting over by Jump Off Joe."

He said this while staring straight ahead, his expression unreadable. But Daisy's heart somersaulted in her chest. Jump Off Joe was an enormous rock that jutted out over the deepest part of the Marietta river. It was also one of the most beautiful stretches and had been their favorite place to swim as kids.

"Oh?" She tried sounding casual. Like she didn't even remember Jump Off Joe. And how much they'd made out there. *Rock? What rock?*

They turned onto the highway and drove most of the way in silence. Daisy watched the farms and ranches whizzing by. The purple mountain range in the distance stood boldly against the Montana heavens that were now swirling pink and orange in the east. Up ahead, a tractor was plowing a rolling field, and plumes of dust rose behind it like smoke. They passed a few trucks on the highway, but not many—mostly semis that had just made their way down the mountain, their brakes smelling hot and tangy from the effort.

She leaned her head back against the rest, enjoying the world outside her window. Boston was beautiful, but it didn't have views like this. Like Mother Nature had paused with her paintbrush and taken a little extra time here.

After about fifteen minutes, they turned off onto a narrow dirt road that wound through a grove of quaking aspen for about a quarter of a mile. And then they were finally at the river and Jump Off Joe, its mossy hulk jutting out over water that was as still and clear as glass.

Daisy smiled as she unhooked her seat belt and climbed out of the truck. The morning was crisp, but she knew the day was going to be hot, even hotter than yesterday, and she was glad she had a thin tank top on underneath her hoodie. She pulled the impossibly sweet river air into her lungs and wondered how she'd managed to live without it all these years. At one point in her life, it had been as important to her as food, as sleep. She seemed to need it as much for her body, as for her soul. But somewhere along the line, she'd pushed it away, along with all the other things she'd needed and had made herself forget. Which had been the safe thing to do. Which was so *her*.

She glanced over at Brooks, who was watching her with a knowing smile.

"You've missed it, haven't you?" he said.

"It's that obvious?"

He grabbed the tackle box and handed her a fishing pole, before they began making their way toward Jump Off Joe with the river gurgling a few yards away. The sun was just now peeking its golden head over Copper Mountain in the distance, and warm, dappled light filtered through the aspen overhead.

They climbed onto the top of the rock, where Brooks put the tackle box down. Daisy sat, scooted up to the edge, and dangled her feet over the water.

"What are we using for bait?" she asked, reaching for her pole.

"Night crawlers."

She wrinkled her nose. As much as she used to love fishing, she'd never gotten used to putting a worm on her own hook.

He smiled. "Don't worry. I'll do it."

"I guess I'm still a wuss."

"I know you're perfectly able, you just don't want to. There's a difference."

"I should learn though, right?"

He shrugged, not looking too concerned either way. But all of a sudden, Daisy wanted to do it herself. Baiting a hook might be a small thing to someone else, and she supposed in the scheme of things it absolutely was. But to her, this morning, it felt important.

She held her hand out. "Worm me."

He looked skeptical. "Are you sure?"

"Better do it before I change my mind."

He handed over the plastic cup with the worms inside. Without letting herself think about it, Daisy popped open the lid, and retrieved a cool, wiggly night crawler.

With surprising efficiency, she stuck the worm on the hook without gagging. "Sorry, worm."

Brooks laughed. "He's fulfilling his destiny. And he'll be responsible for feeding a dude ranch full of guests tonight. It's the circle of life."

Dropping her line in the water, she took a deep breath and pushed her cap up on her forehead. *He's right*, she thought. *I have missed this.* She closed her eyes and tilted her face toward the sun. Brooks plopped his line in the water, too, and settled himself next to her. He smelled good this morning, like deodorant and sunscreen.

She opened her eyes again to gaze down at the water. It was so clear that it was like looking through a jelly jar to the smooth, round river rock at the bottom. There were tiny minnows darting underneath the surface, and she knew it wouldn't be long before they got a nibble.

They both sat there, quiet, listening to the sounds of the river, of the breeze blowing through the aspen above. The leaves rustled gently, lulling her, making her sleepy.

"Did Alex ever take you fishing?"

Daisy startled at the sound of Brooks's voice. But maybe it wasn't so much his voice, as the mention of Alex's name— something that might as well have been a thunderbolt in a clear blue sky.

"Fishing?" She was stalling, but she couldn't help it. Talking about Alex, in any capacity, was dangerous. And this peaceful moment would vanish if they weren't careful.

Brooks pulled his cap down low. He didn't look at her. Just continued watching the tip of his fishing pole. "Fishing," he said. "Did he ever take you?"

"Well, no… That would have to be a hard no."

"Why?"

"He was always so busy with work. There was never a good time."

She snuck another look at him and saw that he was glowering down at the water. The expression on his face was dark, and she shifted her weight on the rock, suddenly fidgety. They hadn't talked about Alex before. At least, not in depth. They'd broken up, Alex had come into the picture a few weeks later, and the rest was history.

She chewed on her bottom lip for a second, trying to decide what to say next. Then, just settled on the truth.

"For what it's worth," she said, "he felt bad about how

things ended up between you two."

At that, Brooks looked over sharply. His hazel eyes were almost black underneath the cap. "What?"

Okay. Maybe it was a little too soon for that kind of truth. She watched him, intimidated by his mood. Angry, brooding. Accusatory.

"He wasn't proud of himself," she said.

"I'd hope not. Since he stabbed me right between the shoulder blades."

She couldn't argue with that. She'd done the same. It was the true that they'd been broken up, and she'd had her reasons at the time. But now, looking back, she had to wonder if she'd just wanted to hurt him, like he'd hurt her.

Brooks glared at the river. "Let's just drop it."

"We were so young, Brooks."

"I told you," he said, his voice low. "I'm over it."

They sat there in silence, as the river flowed lazily below. The sun was starting to warm Daisy's shoulders, but she couldn't bring herself to enjoy it. It felt spoiled now.

"But here's the thing..." Brooks turned to her again. "Why the *hell* did you do it, Daisy?"

"I told you—"

"Yeah, I know. I wasn't ready to settle down."

She shook her head. "No, you didn't say you weren't ready. You said it wasn't for you. You said you didn't want to. Ever."

"And with Alex? *Alex?*"

"Maybe that was just my mic-drop moment. Or something."

"Hell of a mic drop."

"I needed to leave," she said. "I needed to find my way. Away from Mama, away from you. Back then, it felt like I was never going to heal in Marietta."

"I loved you, damn it."

The impact was immediate. She wanted to reach for him. To touch his face and make him understand. But she couldn't, because she didn't understand it all herself.

"I loved you, too," she answered softly. "I can't really explain how much. Even today. Even with all this time between us."

"I would've done anything for you."

She frowned, looking over at his hands, one tucked between his jean-clad thighs, the other holding loosely onto his fishing pole. Remembering again, how they'd felt on her body. Gentle, possessive. Strong and sure.

"Except marry me." *Same old fight...*

"Good God, woman. How many times did I have to say it? Things were great between us. A piece of paper wasn't going to change anything."

"You knew my dad left. That he wouldn't commit to my mom."

"And you knew that I watched my parents' marriage disintegrate."

She looked back at the river, at the thousands of golden

sparkles scattered over its surface. "We wouldn't have ended up like that."

"How do you know?"

"I just do."

"Easy to say now. Now that it's just a hypothetical." He yanked in his line to cast it out again. "You know what I think? I think you were scared. Too scared to stick around and see what might happen with us."

"I never said I wasn't."

"And I think you've been running this whole time. With your tail between your legs, from one mistake, to the next."

She bristled. It was one thing for her to say it. Another thing for him to.

"Okay," she said, scowling over at him. "That's fair. But you're no picture of bravery either, Brooks."

"Oh, really?"

"If you'd truly loved me, you would've given us a chance."

"You mean, given marriage a chance. An institution I don't believe in."

"Still?"

"Still."

"Well, that's too bad."

"Because?"

"Because," she said, "you're going to end up missing out on a nice life with someone. Kids, a family..."

"I'm good. Thanks, though."

She yanked her cap down over her eyes, telling herself she was done with this conversation. He was just baiting her now.

"You used to be so fearless," he said, his voice low. Almost under his breath.

"You act like I'm completely different now. I'm not."

"Oh, yeah?"

"Yes."

"Prove it."

She looked over at him. "I'm sorry?"

"You heard me."

"This is ridiculous. I don't have to prove anything to you."

"Because you know I'm right."

"Let's just for a second pretend you were right. How in the world could I prove it? By doing what?"

He glared at his fishing pole.

She watched him, but he wouldn't look at her. *You used to be fearless...* The words went around and around in her head, until she felt her blood warm in her veins. He was right. She had been fearless. She'd proposed to him, after all. She'd been precocious and wild and unafraid of any kind of consequence—part of the reason why the thought of marriage at eighteen hadn't phased her. She'd simply lived her life the way her mother hadn't, trying her best to be as different as possible.

Since then, she'd grown and changed. Part of that

change had been inevitable; it had needed to happen. But she wished she could've taken some of that wildness with her. Some of that fearlessness. Maybe then she wouldn't have stayed in an unhappy marriage for as long as she had. Maybe she would've come home sooner, when it could've made a difference.

The soft breeze ruffled her ponytail, caressed her face like a long-lost lover. She felt her heart beating inside of her, seeming to repeat the word Brooks had uttered just a minute before. *Fearless, fearless, fearless…*

She looked over at the river, so noble in its never-ending quest to reach the ocean. Then up at the sky, which stretched above them, aspiring to be even bigger than Montana herself, which was a tall order.

Without letting herself think about it, she yanked her cap off and tossed it aside. Then pulled her fishing pole out of the water.

Brooks glanced over. "What are you doing?"

She ignored him and stood to take off her boots.

He frowned. "What the hell are you doing?"

She ignored that, too. When her boots were off, she went to work on her jeans—unbuttoning them and working them over her hips.

Brooks stared at her, his mouth hanging open. His dark gaze fell to her stomach as she pulled her hoodie over her head and dropped it neatly at her bare feet.

She planted her hands on her hips and smiled down at

him. Her underwear and bra even matched this morning, a rarity. He was speechless, she could tell. Which was exactly what she'd been going for.

"Scared, huh?" she said. "Let's see who's scared."

Not giving him time to answer, she stepped up to the edge of their favorite diving spot as kids and jumped.

She hit the icy water with an impressive splash, and the shock of it stole the air from her lungs. She kicked her way to the surface, breaking through with a gasp.

"Have you lost your mind?"

She pivoted in the water and looked up at Brooks, who was standing on the edge of the rock peering back. She brushed her dripping hair away from her face and laughed, unable to help it. In fact, he looked so confused, so completely flummoxed, that she laughed even harder.

"What's so funny?"

"You," she said.

"Me?"

"What's the matter? Didn't see that coming?"

"You're nuts."

She continued treading water, slowly getting used to the temperature. "What you call nuts, I call *fun*."

"So, I guess this is your way of proving it."

"Exactly."

"Nice," he said. "Very nice."

"Now it's your turn."

"No way in hell."

"Why not? You used to do a pretty mean cannonball if I remember correctly."

He shook his head.

"Here's the thing…" she said, floating on her back and looking up at the sky. The water lapped around her ears. "The way I see it, you're between a rock and a hard place."

"How's that?"

"You don't jump in, I get to hold it over you. You do jump in, and you have to ride home in soggy underwear. Either way, I win."

"From where I'm standing, it looks like you're going to have soggy underwear, too."

"Yes, but I'll still be able to hold it over you."

She grinned at the sky, enjoying the moment. Remembering how playful, competitive banter just like this had once led to a fiery relationship. One where jumping in the river fully clothed hadn't been that unusual.

"It's okay if you're scared," she said, lifting her head out of the water to eye him. "I get it."

"Scared?"

"Yeah, scared."

"That's it." He swiped his trucker cap off, making his dark hair stick straight up. "That's *it*."

She watched as he pulled his sweatshirt off and threw it in a pile next to her clothes. His body was hard as a rock in the early morning sunlight, his muscles sliding underneath smooth, tanned skin. He unbuttoned his jeans and dropped them next to the hoodie. Despite the temperature of the water, she warmed at the sight of him in his stark-white boxer briefs. *Good Lord...*

"I'm coming in, so you'd better watch out." He stretched his arm across his chest in his best Clark Griswold impression from *Vacation*. "This is crazy, this is crazy, this is crazy. One...two..."

She laughed, and dog paddled backward, knowing he was going to jump as close as possible to maximize the splash.

"Three!"

He took a couple of steps, and then launched himself in the air. She screwed her eyes shut and looked away, bracing herself for impact. He hit like a ton of bricks, and a wall of water washed over her head.

Wiping her eyes, she looked over as he resurfaced and shook his head like a dog. Droplets of water went flying, and she laughed again, hardly able to believe they were swimming in their underwear. If she didn't have the beginnings of crow's feet to prove otherwise, she'd almost swear they were teenagers again.

She paddled over to the side of Jump Off Joe and grabbed onto it. Underneath her there was a natural bench where the rock jutted out, and she settled herself there, the water lapping around the swell of her breasts.

Brooks swam over, his long, muscular arms moving him through the water like a knife. He'd always been a strong swimmer and had actually been the one to teach her.

He came up next to her and grabbed onto the rock. Water streamed off his dark hair and down his neck. It beaded on his shoulders—tiny pearls of clarity that caught the morning light like stars.

"How's that for scared?" he asked, grinning.

"Okay. I'll give you that one."

"Now we're even."

"I guess. However, technically, I jumped in first."

"Technically."

She smiled and looked away as a peaceful quiet settled over them. For a minute, it was just the sound of the water lapping against their bodies, of the birds chirping to each other in the aspen, of the breeze, soft and insistent through the grass on the banks of the river. For a minute, it felt like they'd never left here. Like she'd never gone to Boston and changed the trajectory of her entire life. And his, too. It felt like they'd been here this whole time, growing older underneath the cool shadow of Jump Off Joe, and watching clouds sail across a sky so blue, it hurt to look at it.

Brooks tipped his head toward her. The water lapped over his chest and back down again, leaving it glistening in the sun. "What are you thinking about?" he asked.

"Nothing."

He was skeptical, she could tell.

"Okay," she said. "That's not true. I was thinking about us."

"What about us?"

She took a breath, concentrating on the cold resistance of the water around her body, and how it ebbed and flowed like waves in the ocean. Of the feel of the rock underneath her bottom, cradling her just right, like a chair carved out by the river itself.

"I was thinking how easy it was to slip back into this. I thought being around you was going to be hard. And it is in a way. But it's easy, too. That part surprises me."

He watched her, his wide, expressive mouth curving on one side. "It shouldn't. We never really had to work at it."

"We didn't have to work at anything."

"Except the staying together part."

His gaze darkened, and then slipped down to where the water pooled between her breasts. It felt as heavy and warm there as one of his hands might. Cupping her, holding her close. When he looked back up, there was an expression on his face that she recognized as a mixture of hunger and pain.

"We were good together, Daisy," he said.

"I know."

"It didn't have to end the way it did."

"I'm not so sure," she said quietly. "I'm better than I was. And I needed to leave to grow into that person."

"I liked the person you were."

"My mom didn't seem to. Not so much."

"She wasn't good to you."

"But she was still my mom." She felt like if she said it

enough, her childhood might start making sense. The cookbook helped. It was a window into her mother's soul—a place she hadn't been able to go as a girl, but now she had a front-row seat. She felt like she was in a darkened movie theater and the lights were beginning to dim. She had no idea what she was about to see, but she was ready.

"I get how you feel," he said. "There were a few years when I didn't think my dad and I would ever talk again, let alone have any kind of relationship."

"And now?"

"Now, he's here. He moved to be close to us. It's a start."

She nodded, absorbing this. She remembered how complicated it had been between them growing up. She'd also seen how happy Eddie was to be in Marietta. How well he was fitting in. Definitely a good start.

"Speaking of," she said. "I went into your dad's shop the other night…"

He raised his brows.

"He was advertising lessons," she continued, "and I just went in. I hadn't planned on it."

"And?"

"*Annnd*, he's going to teach me how to play guitar."

Brooks stared at her.

"What?"

"Nothing. I'm just surprised, that's all."

"You know I always wanted to learn how to play."

"But my dad teaching you?"

"What's wrong with that?"

"You haven't spent much time with my dad," he said dryly. "He's going to tell you all about my love life, at *length*. And probably everyone else's love life who lives within a five-block radius. It's his favorite thing."

"Gossiping?"

"He has a huge piehole."

She laughed.

"I'm glad this is entertaining for you."

"I'm sorry."

"No, you're not."

"Okay, I'm not."

He scowled at her.

"It's just that it's hard to believe," she said. "He's this rock star…"

"He's a little old lady in snakeskin pants."

She sighed, her stomach sore from laughing, then looked up at their discarded fishing poles hanging over the rock. "You promised Owen fish tonight," she said. "Now what?"

"There's still time to catch some."

But they both knew they'd scared away whatever had been swimming underneath the glassy surface before. And the sun was getting warmer by the second. Their fishing window had already closed.

"There's always Monroe's," she said innocently.

He shook his head. "No way. It has to be from the river."

"I'm just saying, nobody would know."

"*I'd* know. And Porter would know. I don't know how, but he would."

Porter did seem pretty perceptive. She thought about what he'd said the other morning when she'd burned her fingers. *You're probably still crazy about each other...*

It would be easy to believe she'd never fallen out of love with Brooks. Easy to pretend the last ten years had never happened. But if she'd learned anything while she was away, it was that she never got anywhere by pretending. They could still have fun together, still rib each other, that was obvious. But anything other than that, Brooks needed to be a sweet memory.

She pushed off the rock and let her body weight sink into the water again. Her legs brushed his as she swam past.

He pivoted toward her. "Where are you going?"

"To get out. I'm getting cold."

She paddled to the riverbank and found her footing on the slippery river rock. Covering her breasts, she glanced back at him. Her bra was flimsy and soaking wet. And basically see-through.

He turned away. "I won't look."

When she was satisfied he'd keep his word, she stepped carefully out of the water, the rocks sharp underneath her tender feet. There was a time when she went barefoot most of the summer. Now, though, she felt every jagged edge as if they had a personal vendetta against her.

"Ouch," she muttered. "Ooh, *ooh*."

She made her way back up Jump Off Joe, the sun warm on her skin. She'd have to sit for a few minutes to dry off. Maybe get a little color while she was at it.

She spread her hoodie out and sat down, looking back out at Brooks. He appeared to have been a perfect gentleman, and was still treading water, facing the other direction.

"Okay. You can look now."

He swam back toward the shore and climbed out, the river water dripping from his body. She looked away, since his boxer briefs were even thinner than her bra, and listened as he made his way up the rock, sucking in a few breaths as he went.

"Damn, that hurts."

He sat down next to her, tipped his face toward the sun, and closed his eyes. "You do realize you were shy about getting out, but now you're sunbathing in your undies?"

"I'm drying off. There's a difference. Besides, I'm not crazy about you seeing me walk away. Too much jiggle."

He smiled, his eyes still closed. "Watching you walk away was the best view I've had all day."

"You weren't supposed to look!" She'd really had no reason to believe Brooks had noticed her physically since she'd been back. There'd been a few glances here and there, but she'd chalked that up to a guy being a guy. This was the first time she had to wonder if he might be feeling anything close to what she was.

She stuck her legs out in front of her and leaned back on

her hands. She wanted to soak in the warmth, soak in the moment. It wouldn't last. It couldn't. Pretty soon, they'd head back toward the ranch, and whatever they'd shared here this morning would be just a memory, along with everything else.

"What was it like growing up with a famous dad?" she asked suddenly. She'd asked him before, of course, when they'd been kids. But either she'd never understood the answer, or he hadn't been able to word it in a way that helped her understand. Either way, she knew they were better able to communicate now, and it was a question that had always nagged at her.

He pulled in a breath. Then let it out slowly. "It was…"

She squinted over at him in the sunlight, shielding her eyes with her hand.

"Lonely…" he finished after a few seconds. "It was really lonely."

She frowned, waiting for him to go on.

He looked over at her. "My brothers and I felt like an afterthought. Something that needed to be set aside for his career. And I'm not blaming him, he did the best he could. My mom didn't give a shit about us. He was only doing what he thought made sense at the time."

"Are you glad he sent you here?"

He smiled at that. "What do you think?"

She smiled back.

"I don't know who I'd be if it weren't for Marietta," he

went on. "But that time we missed with him…we'll never get that back. It's bittersweet."

She nodded, gazing out at the river. Bittersweet was a sentiment she understood. It encapsulated how she felt about her own mother. Although, most days the bitter outweighed the sweet.

"I know I used to have a chip on my shoulder," he said. "I was pissed so often, that by the time I turned eighteen, I'd forgotten who I was supposed to be mad at."

Another thing she understood. To the core. "Me, too," she said softly.

"We had that in common."

"But you dealt with it better than I did. Look at you and your dad now."

"Well, it's not perfect, by any stretch. But we're getting there."

Daisy pulled in a breath. How she wished she could go back and do things differently. Sometimes if felt like that was the hardest part of losing her mother. The regret. The longing for what might've been.

She looked over at Brooks, her throat tightening in that familiar way. "How did you do it?" she asked.

"How did I do what?"

"Forgive him."

His expression softened. Maybe it was because he could see the pain etched on her face. She had a hard time hiding it.

"It took a long, long time, Daisy," he said. "I had to get to know him again. To be able to understand the choices he made. It wasn't him I was really mad at, deep down. It was my mom. He was just the most convenient target."

That made sense. And for the very first time, she could see the parallels to her own childhood. Her dad had left, too. She'd been mad at her mom, too. And her mother had weathered the brunt of that anger, that pain. Not only had Lou Hudson had to absorb her own sorrow at being left, but she'd had to absorb her daughter's as well.

Brooks reached up and ran his knuckles along Daisy's cheek. It was only then that she realized she was crying.

"Oh…" She sniffed, not knowing what to say. Embarrassed that she'd let her guard down in front of him.

"I know you're struggling with how to feel about your mom now," he said quietly. "I'm not saying I get all of it, because I'm too close to be objective. But I do know you shouldn't blame yourself for how you felt then, Daisy. Your relationship with her was complicated. I don't know much, but I do know that."

The tears were coming in earnest now. They slid down her cheeks, one after the other. She'd spent so much time feeling guilty, that it was like what Brooks had just said—she had a hard time remembering who was to blame for what.

He tucked a damp strand of hair behind her ears, and she reached up to grab his wrist.

"Why are you being so nice to me?" she managed.

"Because I think you could use some kindness right now."

He smelled warm and earthy, like the river. His lips, which had been hard that very first day at the ranch, were now relaxed, more pliant.

Her gaze dropped to his neck where she could see his pulse tapping. Water droplets still beaded his skin, which was turning a deeper brown underneath the sun.

Holding onto his wrist, she closed her eyes and rubbed her thumb over it, feeling the coarse little hairs there, the thickness of his muscle and bone. When she opened them again, he was looking at her in a way that slowed her heartbeat in her chest.

"Maybe this wasn't such a good idea," he murmured.

"What wasn't a good idea?" Although, she knew exactly what he meant. *This.* Coming here to their spot on the river and slipping back in time. Or falling back in time was probably a better way to put it. Falling so hard and fast, Daisy hadn't seen it coming. But maybe she simply hadn't *wanted* to see it coming, because then the responsible thing would've been to stop it. She had a history with Brooks. And now she worked for him, too. She couldn't afford to mess this up.

He didn't answer. Instead, he leaned close, his gaze pinning her in place. Every single memory she had of Brooks— as an awkward boy, as a teenager, shirtless in the sun, as a young man with only love and fire in his eyes—came rushing back with such intensity, that her head spun.

He hesitated a few inches from her mouth. She felt his breath puff warm and sweet against her lips. She wanted to stop him. She really did, because she knew all about regret. She'd gotten very acquainted with it over the years. But the longing in her heart was simply too great to utter a word.

And then he kissed her. She realized she'd been waiting for this moment for the longest time. Maybe since the day she'd driven away in Alex's Mustang with her life scattered along the two-lane highway behind her. The last time she'd kissed Brooks, they'd been angry. He'd crushed his mouth to hers and she'd nipped him back. Both too furious to give in to what they really wanted, which was to get naked on the banks of this very river.

Now, he was everything he hadn't been that day—gentle and forgiving, coaxing a soft moan from somewhere deep inside her.

He traced her lips with his tongue, then reached up and ran his fingertips along her jawline. She felt the callouses on his skin, born from hours and hours of working with his hands. She marveled at how they could be so rough and so soft at the same time.

He kissed her as the breeze caressed their bodies, drying them in the sun. She kissed him back thinking only of how familiar he felt, how easy this was.

He finally pulled away, but only after her lips were swollen, and her chest was tight. He'd left her breathless and trembling. Just like that last day, only this morning they had so much more to lose.

They watched each other for a long moment, and Daisy bit her cheek. She'd just complicated her situation at the ranch by about a thousand percent, and she knew it.

Apparently, he did too, because he leaned away from her. A shadow settled over his handsome face, and his lips, which had been so soft a minute ago, hardened again.

Running a hand through his hair, he shook his head. "I'm sorry. I don't know where that came from."

Despite everything, her heart sank at that. Here were the consequences. And they'd be quick and merciless.

"I kissed you back," she said. "I'm sorry, too."

"I guess it's being back here. Talking about the past, all of it."

She nodded.

He reached for his hat and jammed it on his head, pulling it low to shade his eyes. The effect was complete—like a wall going up between them.

"I can't do this, Daisy," he said evenly. "I can't go back to where I was before. It took me too long to get right after you left."

She swallowed. Her tongue felt like a wad of cotton between her teeth. "No, of course. I understand. I can't either."

"And we work together now…"

"Brooks, don't explain. I feel the same way."

For a second, the heartache was so overwhelming, that

she wondered how she ever thought she could come back here again. And then she thought of her sister. Her little sister who was about to have a baby, and who needed her. She thought of her mom, who was buried just across town, in a small plot shaded in the afternoon by the most beautiful old evergreen. And she thought of Brooks, who might regret this kiss, but who would definitely end up forgiving her someday. She had to believe that. And if the path forward was painful and rocky? Well, so be it. She'd put her boots back on and negotiate it like a woman who was done taking the easy route.

He watched her, his eyes dark.

"You know what this means," he said.

She pulled in a breath. It meant so many things. *So many.* But she was having a hard time choosing just one at the moment, because all the implications were swirling around with all the memories, and making her feel like she was hanging onto a roller coaster by her fingernails. "What?"

Turning his cap around backward, he looked at his watch. "We're going to have to get the damn fish from Monroe's now."

She stared at him.

And laughed.

Chapter Nine

A good Chardonnay goes with everything.

BROOKS GLANCED OVER at his father who was leaning his head out the passenger's side window of the truck. His shaggy blond hair blew in the wind, the diamond studs in his earlobe, sparkled in the late day sun.

Smiling, Brooks looked back at the highway ahead. They were on their way back from the grocery store where they'd picked up some wine for Daisy's fish dinner that had her darting around the ranch's kitchen in a nervous panic.

When he'd hired her, there had definitely been a part of him that was hoping she'd fail, just so he could gloat a little. But she'd surprised him—bowing up her back and leaning into the challenge like the Daisy he used to know. It had left him wanting to help where he could, so when he'd told her he was going to pick up his dad earlier, he'd asked if she needed anything in town. She'd looked up from the stove, her silky blond hair piled high on her head, and her readers perched precariously on the tip of her nose. *You're a lifesaver!* she'd said. *I forgot the wine.*

It felt dangerously domestic, having her living in his house, and he fought the urge to wonder if she'd been his wife all this time, instead of Alex's, if she would've stayed. If he could have made her happy. It didn't matter, of course. There was no point in revisiting that particular question, but it still bothered him just the same. Or maybe it was that kiss that was bothering him. Burrowing down into the most protected parts of his heart, to freeze there and shatter later, no doubt.

"I can't believe you're giving her guitar lessons," he mumbled, half to himself.

"Excuse me?"

He glanced over at his dad again, whose thinning hair was now defying logic. It was sticking up all over his head from the wind. Too much mousse, apparently. Combined with too much open window.

"Guitar lessons," Brooks said. "I heard."

"Well, you heard right, my boy. That's what I do now, remember?"

"Yeah, but Daisy?"

"I didn't know who she was at first. But even if I had, I'm an equal opportunity music teacher."

Brooks grit his teeth. But it was impossible to stay irritated at the guy. He looked like a cartoon character. He'd dressed up for dinner, wearing a gray silk shirt buttoned only to his sternum, where chains of various thicknesses lay nestled in his chest hair.

"Don't go asking her about Boston, Dad."

"I'm not going to go asking her about Boston. But if Boston happens to come up, I'll listen politely."

Brooks knew better. His father had a way of coaxing information out of people before they even knew what happened. Daisy had no idea what she was stepping into.

He slowed the truck as the sign for Diamond in the Rough came into view, then turned on his blinker out of sheer habit. The highway stretched toward Copper Mountain in the distance looking empty and burnt orange in the early evening light.

The truck rocked over the bumpy lane, and his dad grabbed onto the handle overhead.

"I don't understand why *you* don't want to ask about Boston," he said. "Since there's about a ten-year gap where you could use some filling in."

Brooks stared at the road ahead. "I know all I need to about those ten years."

"And?"

"And she was married to someone else."

"But she's single now. And so are you. And you said yourself she was pretty close to perfect."

"*Was.*" Brooks said. "I said she *was* pretty close to perfect."

"People change, son."

"Yeah, I know. I'm not nearly the sucker I used to be." Technically, that wasn't quite true. He'd kissed her this morning, even though he'd tried his damnedest not to. But his dad didn't have to know that.

His father grunted as they pulled into the gravel driveway. Lily's Jeep was parked next to the barn, and as they got out of the truck, they heard voices carrying from around back.

"Dinner served outside, huh?" his dad said, grabbing the wine. "Nice touch."

They headed toward the picnic table that sat in the shade of a giant sweet gum that had been on the property for two hundred years. The barn in the distance was a regal old lady that added an immeasurable amount of charm to the ranch's ambiance. At the end of every month, Brooks and Porter threw a dance for their guests, and the huge doors, red and peeling, stood open as live country music spilled into the warm summer night.

But tonight the big barn sat quiet, the only music coming from a playlist on Daisy's phone. Lily was helping her carry dishes out from the kitchen, as Porter handed out beers and lemonade. The horses grazed close to the fences and nickered occasionally into the velvety soft air. It was a pretty evening, made prettier by the ranch's cook in the yellow dress who he couldn't take his eyes off of.

Daisy set a basket of bread down on the table and smiled wide when she saw them coming.

"Supper's ready, everyone!"

Again, that undeniable feeling of domestic warmth unfurled inside Brooks's chest. He had to remind himself that she was here because he'd hired her. She was getting paid for this. She wasn't his wife or his girlfriend, or even his partner. She was an employee, and seeing her as anything more, even for a few seconds, would lead to nothing but trouble.

He watched as she gave his dad a hug, then introduced him to Lily and the rest of the group. Of course, there were the usual gasps and requests for autographs when they realized they were meeting Eddie Cole the rock star. But after a few minutes, his father seemed to blend right in. Even in his snakeskin pants, which was a trick.

Daisy showed everyone to the table, where a vase of purple and pink snapdragons sat next to the salad. There was strawberry rhubarb pie for dessert, and it all looked so good that Brooks kept sneaking glances at Daisy, wondering how she'd pulled all this together in a way that made the ranch feel like a home, truly, for the very first time.

He grabbed a chair and sat next to Porter, who gave him a knowing look.

"What?" he mumbled, spreading his napkin in his lap.

"Nothing. Just that she's kind of proving you wrong."

"I never said she wouldn't be good at this."

"You might not have said it, but I know you were thinking it."

"I hired her, didn't I?"

Daisy cleared her throat from across the table. "If any of you don't want fish, there's white cheddar mac and cheese in

that blue dish over there. It was a specialty of my mom's."
She said that last part with a smile, obviously proud of it.

Brooks's chest tightened at the expression on her face. It
was one of peace, of making amends. And it looked good on
her.

Her gaze shifted to meet his, and he smiled, then looked
away, not trusting himself with anything more than that.

Everyone started passing the dishes around, talking in
low tones. Every now and then, laughter would punctuate
the warm evening air, and Brooks glanced around. A few of
the tech employees were talking to his dad about his first
album, *Mistletoe Magic*. One of them announced he knew
every word to every song and proved it by breaking into the
lyrics.

Lily was chatting at the other end of the table with one
of the group's female employees about baby names, her
swollen belly making it hard to sit close enough to the table.
Every now and then, she and Daisy would look at each
other, something private passing between them. They'd been
so close growing up, it was hard to believe Daisy had actually
left.

She'd left him, too. A distinct bitterness crept up on him
then. He wondered if he'd ever be able to let it go and move
on from her in a way that was healthy for them both. Or, if
feeling this way meant that he wasn't ready to move on.

Beside him, Porter cut into his trout and took a bite.
Then pointed his fork at Brooks. "And you said you caught

this?" he asked, raising his brows. "This morning?"

Brooks looked down at his plate, busying himself with cutting his own fish. "Yup."

"Huh. Because I ran into Carol Bingley today at Marietta Western Wear..."

Brooks glanced up at Daisy, who was staring back. This wasn't good. Carol Bingley was the town crier. She knew everything about everyone and could spread the word faster than the *New York Post* on steroids.

"And she said she saw you two coming out of Monroe's this morning," Porter finished smugly. "You know. About the time you said you were supposed to be fishing."

Brooks laughed. "I have no idea what you're talking about."

"Really?" Porter popped a bite of buttery trout in his mouth, then washed it down with a long swallow of beer, before going on. "Because she also offered up another interesting detail..."

All at once, the rest of the conversation at the table came to a lull, and everyone fell silent.

Brooks smiled, pretending he didn't have a care in the world.

Owen moaned from across the table after taking a bite of the mac and cheese. "Oh my gerd..." he mumbled, pushing his glasses up. He was the only one who seemed oblivious to the subject of Carol Bingley. "What do you *put* in this?"

Eric Romano, the blowhard Owen couldn't stand, sat

next to him, buttering his bread and looking curiously at Brooks, then Daisy, and back again. Lily was also sitting forward and watching them, her stomach pressed against the picnic table like a beach ball.

Porter grinned, knowing he had everyone's attention now. Even Owen's, who'd just tuned in.

"She said you both looked like you'd been swimming," Porter said. "Which is fascinating, since you'd gone to the river to *fish*. Which means you might not have had time to swim *and* catch dinner?"

Brooks sat lower in his chair, wishing he'd been wearing his Stetson which would've hidden his eyes. It would've been easier to lie that way. Instead, he felt the weight of Porter's maddening smile all the way to his bones. He *knew* his brother would find out about the damn fish. That was bad enough. But the swimming, too? He silently cursed Carol Bingley and her giant mouth.

"*Somebody* caught it," he mumbled. "It just wasn't…us."

Porter laughed and slapped the table. "I knew it! I can always taste freshly caught trout. Don't you know that by now?"

"I do. I knew you'd know."

"Good. Now you know that I know."

The guests laughed, now fully on board with the ribbing.

"Well, I don't care where you got it," Owen said. "It's so good."

Brooks nodded toward Daisy. "Monroe's sells great fish,

but they can't take the credit for cooking it. All that goes to Daisy here."

Everyone started clapping, and Daisy's cheeks colored. Smiling, she lowered her lashes. He could tell she was enjoying this.

Porter leaned close. "I'll be expecting details about the swimming part later."

Brooks took a bite of bread so he wouldn't have to answer.

"I'd like to make a toast," Lily said, and raised her glass of lemonade. "To my big sister… I'm so happy you're home. Cheers."

Everyone raised their glasses. "Cheers!"

Brooks took a long swallow of his beer, watching Daisy as he licked the tanginess from his lips. She was home. But for how long? How long would this last? She'd cut and run the last time things got hard. Why wouldn't she do the same thing again? Of course, this time it would be easier. He'd just have a cook to replace, not the love of his life.

Still, even as he sat there thinking it, he knew it wouldn't be that simple. Daisy had come back into his world and had tilted it on its axis. He'd been trying hard not to let her affect him, but it was like trying to hold back the tide. Every time he looked at her, wave after wave of memories washed over him. Emotions, old and new, that he was having to negotiate on an hourly basis. She wasn't the same person who'd left Marietta all those years ago, that was obvious. So what was stopping him from looking inside himself and finding the grace to forgive her?

Honestly, he was afraid if he took that step, if he opened his heart enough to let that old anger go, he'd leave it vulnerable enough to fall for her again, and he didn't think he could survive that. His mother had left. Daisy had left. He was done with being left.

Brooks stared at his plate, pushing the salad around with his fork. All of a sudden, all he wanted to do was take her in his arms and kiss her again. This time, long and slow, with his hands in her hair. Maybe if they just got this over with, whatever was building between them, they'd be able to be done with it once and for all.

"Oh…*oh*! I think he's choking!"

Brooks looked up to see Eric Romano clutching his throat. Owen was pounding on the poor guy's back.

Brooks shoved away from the table. But before he could make his way around it, Daisy was already there. She pulled Eric up by the armpits, and stood behind him, planting her feet apart.

"It's okay," she said. "It's going to be okay."

She wrapped her arms underneath his rib cage and gave him a sharp thrust. She'd always been athletic and strong. But right then, Brooks didn't think he'd ever seen anyone move with such confidence. He froze, watching her.

Eric's eyes bugged as she thrust again. And this time something flew out of his mouth and landed with a plop next to his loafers. He coughed and sputtered.

"Holy crap, man," Porter said, taking him by the arm. "Are you okay?"

Eric nodded and sat heavily. Owen sat beside him, handing him a glass of water. An employee bonding moment from hell.

Daisy looked momentarily dazed, like she couldn't believe what she'd just done. Her hair had come loose from its clip and fell in soft strands around her face.

Eric gazed up at her. "You saved my life."

"Anyone would've done the same," she said, patting his shoulder. "I'm just glad you're okay."

"Where in the world did you learn how to do that?" Lily asked.

"The soup kitchen. It happens sometimes." She leaned down next to Eric. "I hope this doesn't mean you're going to skip the pie. It goes down smoother than the fish, I promise."

Everyone laughed. And just like that, the mood lifted like a balloon into the evening sky. One of the horses whinnied from the pasture, and another answered. The guests settled back at the table as Daisy began cutting fat pieces of pie and putting them on paper plates.

Brooks's dad made his way over, watching Eric take a bite of his dessert. Owen slapped his new frenemy good-naturedly on the back. Softer this time, so as not to break a rib. The two of them had definitely bonded. Maybe it wouldn't last, but it was something. A start. This kind of trip brought people together. Or maybe it was just this place that brought them together. Like magic.

Brooks looked over at Daisy, who was busy making sure everyone was taken care of. Her smile was as sweet as the vine-ripened strawberries she'd baked with, and he had to remind himself that he didn't love her anymore.

"Hey," his dad said, elbowing him in the side. "What were you saying about her not being perfect again?"

Chapter Ten

Don't be afraid to set off the smoke alarm.

D AISY COULDN'T SLEEP. Rolling over, she fluffed her pillow and sighed. Moonlight, a stunning bluish silver, bathed her room in its cool mystique. Stars twinkled outside her open window, glittering against the velvet sky like precious stones. The night air had cooled and felt so good on her skin that she'd kicked her covers off completely.

She gazed out the window now, looking at the stars, and trying to remember what she'd once known about constellations. In Boston the sky was always grainy, like right before dawn. There were just too many city lights to ever get a good look. Out here, so many stars and planets and satellites crowded the heavens, she was surprised there was room for them all.

She smiled, thinking again of dinner, and how she'd pretty much nailed it tonight. She'd surprised herself and had been proud of how it turned out. She knew Brooks had noticed, too, and she couldn't deny being happy about that as well. She'd wanted to impress him. To show him what this job meant to her.

Turning her face into the pillow, she took a deep breath. It smelled fresh, like lavender. The sheets were silky and cool, but she still couldn't get comfortable. Her mind was racing—thoughts bouncing off each other like tennis balls.

She sat up and turned on the vintage lamp beside her bed. As wonderful as tonight had been, as proud as she was that she'd been able to pull it off, she couldn't stop thinking about her mom. Wishing that she could've been there to see it. The cooking part would have made her happy.

Daisy looked over at the old cookbook which sat on the chair by the window. It seemed to be the only connection she had to her mother now. When Daisy had come home to Marietta, she hadn't been prepared for the longing she'd feel for her mom, the desire to know her again. The cookbook had begun to represent something that she didn't fully grasp yet. She only knew that opening it in the morning and closing it at night had become a precious ritual that she seemed to need on a deep, primitive level.

Tucking her hair behind her ears, she climbed out of bed. The hardwood floor was cool underneath her feet as she padded over to pick it up. She cradled it to her chest, careful with the elderly cover, and got back in bed. Setting it on her lap, she ran her fingertips over the word *Joy* in the faded title.

She'd always wondered why her mom had spent such an obsessive amount of time in their cramped little kitchen, experimenting with recipes, swearing under her breath, smiling wide when something turned out just right. To Daisy, it sometimes felt like she'd loved this damn book more than her. But now, through adult's eyes, she was starting to see that her mother's time in the kitchen had been an escape from a life that had turned out to be hard in ways that Daisy hadn't understood as a teenager. Cooking had been a way to keep part of herself alive—the warm part, the romantic part.

Daisy swallowed hard, opening the cookbook to where a faded pink envelope stuck out. There were so many stray papers, it was hard to keep them all in place. She kept telling herself she was going to sit down soon and go through the book page by page, organizing the loose recipe cards and clippings, so she wouldn't lose anything. But there just hadn't been time yet, and she'd limped along so far by keeping a big rubber band around it.

Frowning, she pulled the envelope out and turned it over. Her heartbeat slowed in her chest. She recognized the curve of her own handwriting, the yellowing stamp from years ago. A letter she'd sent to her mom when she'd first moved to Boston. She remembered buying the stationery, which she'd thought looked hopeful and delicate at the time. Not unlike how she'd come to think of those first few years in the city. The letter had been one of the very first she'd sent to her mom. Eventually, they'd dwindled away to nothing but a trickle. She'd been too stubborn to come right out and ask for forgiveness, and her mother had been too stubborn to give it.

Daisy picked the envelope up and turned it over. There, on the back, was a little note her mother had written to herself. A reminder. Maybe to set on the kitchen counter so she'd see it the next day. *Call Daisy*, it said. And then, underneath, *Don't argue. Just tell her you love her.*

She blinked down at the writing, until her eyes blurred with tears. She couldn't remember if she'd gotten that call. Couldn't remember if her mom had told her she loved her. Surely she had. They'd been broken, but they hadn't been that far gone. Had they?

She set the letter in her lap and stared out the window, the sheer white curtain billowing in the midnight breeze. It carried with it the sweet scent of the ranch—the horses and cattle. She breathed deeply, as warm, salty tears dripped from her cheeks onto her collarbone. *Why* had she run away like she had? Why hadn't she come home sooner? Because her mother was complicated? If it had been an excuse before, it wasn't now.

People were complicated and messy. That didn't make it right to cut them out of your life because they no longer fit there conveniently. She'd been looking for a way out in Boston, a way forward that didn't involve the broken relationships in her life. She'd thought Alex was going to mend things for her, when she'd only managed to cut herself more deeply. If she didn't find a way to stop the bleeding soon, she was afraid she was going to lose what was left of herself. And she didn't want to lose herself. She was starting to see a woman worth saving. Someone who'd come home again, after all.

Sniffing, she tucked the letter back into the cookbook again. Like the notes in the margin, the message on the envelope felt like a gift from her mother. Something sent from beyond, when Daisy had needed it the most. Her mom hadn't been much of a nurturer when she was alive. Maybe she'd finally learned some softness on the other side. It was a nice thought.

She set the cookbook down and looked over at the clock on the dresser. Almost twelve thirty. The house was so quiet, she could almost feel it breathing. The walls seemed to sigh as she got out of bed again and reached for her robe. She slipped it on and tied it loosely around her waist. As a kid, warm milk had always done the trick when she couldn't sleep. Lately, she'd had a harder and harder time falling into that blissful place between dreams and wakefulness, where she could sometimes fly if she believed hard enough. Tonight, she knew she'd need some help getting there.

Tiptoeing over to the door, she opened it and looked down the darkened hallway. All the guests' doors were closed, and there wasn't a peep coming from any of their rooms. Not surprising—Brooks and Porter had been keeping them so busy, they usually fell into bed right after dinner, and didn't stir again until morning. Today had been especially tiring, with a late-afternoon horseback ride, and a firepit at dusk. And of course, the drama with poor Eric almost choking to death. She guessed even the night owls were exhausted.

She made her way down the hallway and crept down the stairs. The house was full of moonlight. It flooded in through the windows and spilled onto the living room floor like liquid silver. The towering grandfather clock ticked off the seconds in the living room, each one louder and more accusatory than the one before. She should be asleep with everyone else. Not sneaking into the kitchen for a glass of milk, and probably a chocolate chip cookie if she could scare one up.

Taking a deep breath, she stepped off the staircase and onto the living room floor. The big, dark kitchen yawned to her right, and she tiptoed inside without flipping on the overhead lights.

She walked over to the fridge and opened it up. Cool air whispered against her legs as she leaned in and reached for the carton of milk.

"Can't sleep?"

She jumped, nearly dropping the milk on her toe. "*Wha'?*"

Standing there in a pair of pajama bottoms and no shirt, was Brooks. She blinked up at him, her heart beating in her throat.

"Sorry," he said. "Didn't mean to scare you."

"What are you doing down here?"

"What are *you* doing down here?"

"I was just getting some milk. And having a heart attack."

He smiled, the moonlight playing over his face. "I heard you walk past my room."

"How could you have possibly heard that? I didn't make a sound."

"You *thought* you didn't make a sound." He tapped his head. "I've got ears like a bat."

"Apparently."

She was trying not to look at his naked torso. Trying really, really hard. But her gaze dropped there anyway. His chest was a work of art—thick and sculpted from daily physical labor. His abs were toned in a way that she'd only seen on models in magazines. A dark line of hair ran down his stomach and disappeared below the drawstring on his pajama pants. She couldn't seem to look away.

"You're staring."

She met his gaze again, her ears pulsing. In fact, her entire face felt like it was on fire, and she wished the fridge was open again. She'd probably just climb inside and close the door.

"Excuse me?"

His mouth tilted into a cocky smile. A lot of things had changed about Brooks, but that smile was exactly the same.

"You're staring," he said evenly. "At me."

"I was not."

"Were, too."

"Whatever, Brooks. I'm going back to bed."

She tried stepping around him, but he blocked her way. Still smiling. Still cocky.

"Don't," he said. "I'm sorry. Have your milk."

"I don't want it anymore. You ruined it for me."

"I ruined your milk?"

She glared up at him. Electricity crackled between them. Truth be told, it had started sparking that very first day, when she'd climbed the porch steps to the front door, her knees trembling beneath her. And she'd felt it every day since. But except for the unfortunate fishing expedition yesterday, she'd done a pretty good job of keeping herself in check. Brooks was in her past. They'd already been down this road before, and it had been a dead end.

"Daisy…"

Her heart pounded in her chest. She couldn't remember why she was irritated. He'd been teasing her. And she'd been about to say…what, exactly? It was all a blur now, because all she could concentrate on was the blue moonlight over his skin.

"Brooks," she began. "I don't…"

"I know what you're going to say."

She raised her brows.

"This isn't a good idea," he said. "I know. We covered that yesterday."

"You hate me. You have to hate me. So why did you kiss

me?"

He frowned. And she immediately missed the playful, sexy look on his face that had been there just a second before.

"Hate you?" he asked, his voice husky.

She nodded, not trusting herself to speak. All of a sudden, she felt raw. Raw and vulnerable and scared of where this was going. Kissing each other in the heat of the moment was one thing. This felt like something else. Like they might be headed in a direction that would be harder to come back from.

He stared down at his feet for a second, looking like he was composing himself. She busied herself with taking full breaths, in through her nose and out through her mouth. She was dizzy, light-headed. But it was hard to tell how much of that had to do with this conversation, and how much had to do with Brooks's lack of clothing. If he'd keep his damn shirt on, maybe she'd have a shot at keeping her hands off him for the rest of the summer.

He shook his head. "How can you say that? Is that what you really think?"

"Of course I do."

"No idea," he muttered. "You really have no idea. About anything."

She lifted her chin. She was done dancing around this subject, *and* this man. If they were ever going to move forward, they'd have to deal with this once and for all.

"You said so yourself, Brooks. I mean, basically you did.

The other day, right here in this kitchen."

He stared at her. "I said what?"

"I can't remember your exact words, but you made your point well enough."

He stepped close enough that she could smell the slightest bit of musky aftershave from the day before. She could see the individual points of stubble on his chin. She wanted to reach up and touch it, feel it underneath her fingertips.

"What was I supposed to say, Daisy? Tell you that I've never gotten over you? That our breakup was the hardest thing I've ever had to go through in my life? Or that seeing you again just about broke me in half? Because I wasn't really ready to have that kind of conversation. Still not ready, to be honest. But I can see we're going to keep coming back to this again and again until we do something about it."

"Finally. Something we agree on."

He scowled at her. Then, before she knew what was happening, he reached out and wrapped a muscular arm around her waist. Then pulled her close.

She gasped. "What are you doing?"

"Doing something about it."

"I meant *talk* about it, Brooks."

"We've done enough talking to last a lifetime."

She wanted to fight him. Because she knew what would happen if she didn't. But the problem was, she'd become so obsessed with him touching her, that she couldn't open her mouth to argue. She just stared up at him, waiting for him to take her where she was dying to go.

In one swift move, he picked her up. Then bounced her against his chest for good measure. She wrapped an arm around his neck, and laughed, unable to help it.

"Are you actually carrying me off to bed?"

"Maybe not bed exactly. But bed*room*?"

She felt her smile fade as she looked into his eyes. So dark, so deep, so familiar. "You know this will complicate things, right?"

"Honey, complicated is our middle name."

He stood there for a minute, maybe waiting for her to stop him. Probably expecting her to. But then, when she turned her face into the warm hollow of his throat, he carried her out of the kitchen and toward his bedroom at the base of the stairs.

She knew it wasn't a good idea. But all she wanted right then was to fall into this, fall back to where they'd been ten years ago. It wouldn't last, it couldn't. But she didn't have the strength anymore to fight her longing where Brooks was concerned. She seemed to need him like she needed air or food or water. He was a basic life support system that she'd somehow managed to do without all these years. Which made her a walking, talking miracle.

They came to his bedroom, and he pushed the door open with his foot. The room was spacious and dark, cooler than her room upstairs. Brooks had his window open too, and the curtains moved in the breeze. His Stetson hung on his bedpost, along with his T-shirt, looking incredibly intimate there, and stirring all kinds of desire in her lower belly.

Gently, he set her down on the floor and brushed her hair away from her face.

"Okay," he said, his voice low. "Now that we've had a minute to think about it, maybe you'd better walk out of here before I end up taking you to bed. For real this time."

She smiled up at him. "Want to know something?"

"Hmm."

"That kiss yesterday took me back to a place that I don't want to leave just yet."

His jaw twitched. "Me, neither. But what about tomorrow? What about next week? Are we prepared to deal with the fallout?"

"Meaning, can we sleep together with no strings attached?"

"Right."

That, she didn't know. She'd like to think she was a mature, modern woman who could compartmentalize sex and love, but the fact was, they'd always gone hand in hand for her. What if she slept with Brooks tonight and she fell in love with him again? But that was just dumb, because she'd never fallen out of love with him. So where did that leave her? Denying her feelings, denying her longing, denying everything up to this point.

He reached up and cupped her cheek, and she closed her eyes as he brushed his thumb underneath her eyelashes.

"Want to know what I think?" he said.

She opened her eyes again and looked up at him.

"I think you're probably going to leave again," he finished quietly. "If I'm being honest."

She stared at him. "What do you mean?"

"Daisy. Come on. Do you really see yourself in Marietta for good?"

She stiffened. "Of course I do."

He chuckled, but it was bitter-sounding.

"I left before, Brooks. That doesn't mean I'm going to leave again."

"Even if things get hard? Even if things get messy between us?"

"Okay. I get what you're trying to do here."

He watched her.

"You're trying to sabotage this before it even happens," she continued. "You want me to say I might leave so you can push me away. So you won't have to give in to what you really want. Which might be something more than just one night together."

"Really."

"Really. Want to know what *I* think?"

He looked down at her, infuriatingly handsome and self-confident. He'd always been this way during arguments—cool as a cucumber, while smoke practically puffed out her ears.

"Please," he said. "By all means."

She plowed ahead, ignoring his cockiness, which had come back with a vengeance. How could she have been turned on by that five minutes ago? "I think you're going to be *looking* for reasons for me to leave."

"That's ridiculous."

"Why?"

"I wouldn't need to look for reasons. They're all over the place."

She stomped her foot. Actually stomped her foot. This is what he did to her. "They are not."

"What about Alex?"

"What about him?"

"What if you decide to get back together? I had a hard enough time not killing him before."

"Brooks. Alex isn't part of this scenario anymore."

"Really? Because I'm a guy, Daisy, and I understand how guys think. He's going to realize sooner or later what he lost."

"He never loved me. Not truly. He won't realize anything."

He watched her, and the look on his face right then broke her heart. "How could he *not* have loved you?" he said quietly.

At that, she stepped close, hesitated for just a second, then wrapped her arms around his waist. She tilted her head back to look him in the eyes, her breasts tingling as they brushed against his bare chest.

"I never gave him the chance," she said. "I was in love with someone else."

Before he could open his mouth and say anything more, she stood on her tiptoes and kissed him.

The kiss yesterday had been impulsive, unplanned. This one had teetered almost unbearably on the edge of her lips for the last twenty-four hours.

He stiffened, his body hard and unyielding against hers. The subject of Alex having come between them like it always did. But after a few seconds, he relaxed, and then reached up to wrap his hands in her hair.

His mouth moved over hers, gently at first, then rougher, hungrier. She responded by pressing herself closer. It no longer mattered what the consequences were. She didn't care if they broke her into a thousand sparkly shards. She just wanted to be kissed long and deep by the one man she'd never let herself forget.

He picked her up, and this time, carried her to his bed. So many memories came back to her then, like fish swimming upstream to where they'd been born. These memories didn't have to struggle against the current, though. It swept them toward her, where she waited with open arms. With an open heart.

He lay her down on the bed, and she settled there like she'd meant for this all along. Moving underneath him in an erotic dance as old as time herself. This was what love felt like. This was what life felt like, when she finally let herself live it.

Easing himself over her, he paused a few inches above her mouth. She stared up at him, wondering how long it would be until he broke her heart again. And despite herself, wondering how long it would be until she *was* tempted to leave Marietta. He was right. When things got hard, she ran. What was so different this time?

Slowly, he leaned down and pressed his lips to hers.

Everything, she told herself. Everything was different this time.

Chapter Eleven

If life give you lemons, make lemonade! (And store them in the fridge until you do. They'll keep longer.)

DAISY WALKED INTO Mistletoe Music a full ten minutes before her lesson. Mostly because she'd been so nervous about it, that she'd left the ranch in Brooks's truck convinced she was already late. But she'd forgotten how little traffic there was in Marietta in the evenings, so she was early, and actually had time to savor the little things now, like the anticipation and excitement of starting something new.

The shop was full of people browsing—testing out the glossy guitars and admiring the blocky drum sets. A couple of employees were busy helping folks out, but Daisy didn't spot Eddie anywhere, so she walked over to the old staircase to get a closer look at one of his platinum albums on the wall.

She could hardly believe she was about to take her first guitar lesson from Eddie Cole himself. It was tantamount to taking ballet lessons from Misty Copeland, and butterflies tickled her rib cage. But honestly, she didn't know how much of that had to do with her lesson, or how much had to do with how entangled she was becoming with the Coles again. Once upon a time, she'd been Brooks's girlfriend. Now, she was working for him. And sleeping with him too, apparently. Let's not forget that. As if she could.

Studying the album on the brick wall, she ran her tongue over her chapped lips. They were chapped from kissing. From hours and hours of kissing the other night. She and Brooks hadn't just made love in his bedroom under that impossible moon. They'd made out like teenagers.

Something wet brushed her ankle. Startling, she looked down to see an impossibly fat Chihuahua gazing back. It blinked up at her through watery eyes. Then licked her again for good measure.

"That's Buddy Holly," said a smooth voice behind her. "And you'd better watch that tongue, because the next thing you know, it'll be in your ear."

Daisy grinned and turned to Eddie, who was standing there with his arms crossed over his chest. He wore another silk shirt today, this one leopard print, and tight black leather pants. His rings sparkled underneath the shop lighting, trying their best to outdo the sparkle of the chains around his neck. He could pull it off. Eddie Cole was *meant* to sparkle.

"He's adorable," she said, looking back down at the dog. "*So* cute." She bent to scratch his bottom, and he closed his buggy eyes in canine contentment.

"He knows it, too."

"Is he yours?"

"God no. I don't do small creatures. They need too much nurturing, and I'm, well…me. He belongs to Nathan over there." He nodded in the direction of a twenty-something guy with a green mohawk. He was ringing someone up at the cash register, but when he heard his name, he waved.

Straightening, Daisy waved back.

"You all set?" Eddie asked. "I've got the prettiest little Fender with your name all over it."

Her heart squeezed when she looked into the small room where two guitars sat waiting. One of them was the guitar she'd seen in the window that first night—the night she'd decided to come in and ask about lessons. It was so beautiful, it took her breath away.

"All set," she said. "I'm so excited. I've been wanting to do this for a long time."

"I know you have. And just for the record, we'll stick to the music. I won't try and find out if you're in the market for a relationship or anything."

"I…"

"Brooks," he continued. "I'm under strict orders."

She laughed. "Ahh. Well, don't worry. We won't tell him."

"But I can't promise I won't dig a little. Since I'm a dad, and he's my boy. And I can tell he's head over heels for you, darling."

She felt her cheeks warm at that. She wasn't sure it was true. Brooks *used* to be head over heels, but it was nice to hear just the same. She'd spent the last few days convincing herself that what happened the other night, probably wouldn't happen again. But every time she thought she'd put Brooks into the one-night stand category, the *this was fun, but it definitely won't happen again* category, her heart lurched, reminding her that she wasn't fooling anyone. She loved Brooks. She'd always loved Brooks. Now, she just had to figure out how she was going to live with that.

The little bell above the door tinkled as someone walked in, bringing with them a sweet cloud of perfumed air.

Daisy turned. And when her gaze settled on the woman with the long, dark hair and rhinestone belt buckle, her stomach dropped.

"Oh, shit," she muttered, and dipped her head.

Eddie glanced around. "What?"

"Nothing." She resisted the urge to grab his silky sleeve and drag him into the lesson room before the woman recognized her.

"Daisy?"

She froze. Then slowly looked up and plastered on her friendliest smile. But it wasn't easy. She couldn't stand Kylee Turner. The other woman had always had a thing for Brooks, and a particular disdain for Daisy. She knew Kylee and Brooks had dated briefly, thanks to the magic of small-town information spreading like a grass fire in July. She also knew Kylee had been bad-mouthing her to anyone who would listen.

It didn't matter. Daisy hadn't come home again thinking everyone would be happy to see her. On the contrary. She'd prepared herself for just this type of encounter.

"Kylee," she said. "How are you? It's been a long time."

Kylee smiled back, cat-like and chilly. "Ten years," she said. "Or coming up on that."

"What have you been up to? Do you still rodeo?"

"Sure do. Was Copper Mountain Rodeo Queen last year. And the year before that."

She looked like a rodeo queen. She glittered from the toes up, and was so pretty, you kind of had to stare. Which was exactly what Eddie was doing.

Daisy cleared her throat. "I'm sure you know Eddie, Brooks's dad?"

Kylee's ruby-red lips stretched wider. She batted her eye-lashes and extended a slender hand. "We haven't met officially, but I sure know who you are, Mr. Cole. It's a pleasure."

"The pleasure's all mine," Eddie said.

"I used to date Brooks." She gave Daisy a look. "But we decided to take a little break."

Daisy grit her teeth. Really, it was a break*up*, but whatev-er. Brooks probably had a long and colorful dating history in Marietta, and she could live her entire life without knowing any of the details.

"Well, we'll have to tell him we ran into you," Eddie said. "He's up to his eyeballs in dude ranching at the moment. Lucky that Daisy here came along when she did, or he would've been stuck cooking himself, and that wouldn't have been pretty."

Kylee's smile faded. "Isn't that nice."

Eddie's support was so subtle, Daisy doubted anyone else would've been able to pick up on it, but she felt it to her core. He was making sure Kylee knew where she fit in the scheme of things. And even if it was just an employee, it was still a part of Brooks's daily life, and that was probably more than Kylee would like. Judging by the expression on her face.

Her green eyes narrowed a little. "I'm surprised you were interested in that position, Daisy," she said. "I heard you were pretty spoiled in Boston. You know. Before the divorce."

Daisy wasn't going to let that rattle her. She just wasn't. If little jabs like that were going to make Kylee feel better, well, then. Let her have her fun.

"I'm happy to have it," she said. "It's hard work, but I'm learning a lot." *And I never was above anything, despite what you might think.*

Kylee held a finger to her lips and tapped them as if she were thinking. "Wasn't your mom the cook in the family? I seem to remember some pie baking contests, or something like that. So cute. But I know after you left, she had to do something to keep busy."

Daisy's ears began to throb. She reminded herself that this woman knew nothing about her mother, or her relationship with her mother, or anything about her life, for that matter. As catty as Kylee was, she had to cut her some slack. Brooks had broken her heart, and Daisy was in a unique position to know exactly how that felt. Brooks saying goodbye was fairly life-altering.

"She was an amazing cook," Daisy said. "Pies were her specialty."

Kylee nodded, her glossy mane falling over one shoulder. "And how's Alex doing?" she asked. "You know, I heard he's back in town…"

Daisy froze. "I'm sorry?"

Kylee smirked, enjoying the fact that she'd hit her intended target. Even though it was kind of like hitting a dart board with a bazooka gun. Not a lot of skill involved.

"Alex. He's back in town. His sister still lives in Marietta, but you had to know that."

She did know that. But Alex hadn't spoken to her in years. After his parents died, they'd grown apart, although he and Daisy would still get an occasional Christmas card. Alex's leaving Marietta hadn't affected him like it had his new wife. He'd detached himself from his childhood with almost surgical precision. He'd always believed he'd been meant for bigger things, and his ability to compartmentalize his emotions had been another thing that had come between them in their marriage. He wasn't cold, but he was calculating. And he knew exactly what he wanted—the girl he'd set his sights on after high school, the nice apartment, the fancy car, the career that didn't leave much time for anything else.

So, the fact that he was back did surprise her. She thought he'd washed his hands of Montana a long time ago.

Kylee watched her. "I'm sure he'll track you down eventually," she said. "Maybe he'll want to work things out. You know how it goes."

"I don't think so. Our divorce is final. He's moved on and so have I."

But saying it and believing it were two different things. Alex was like a bulldog when he sunk his teeth into something. Whatever brought him back home was important to him, she was sure of it. There was a good reason. All of a sudden, her stomach felt sick.

Kylee tossed her hair back and smiled. Her teeth flashed against her flawless, olive skin. "Well, just be glad he's not tracking Brooks down." She laughed. "*That* wouldn't end well, would it?"

No. No, it wouldn't.

Chapter Twelve

Use cayenne pepper to pack an extra punch.

BROOKS LED BASIL, his old Appaloosa gelding, toward a shady turnout by the barn—the one next to the apple tree that dropped its ripest treasures within eating distance. It was Basil's most cherished spot these days, and who was Brooks to deny him anything at this point?

He reached up and patted the horse's spotted neck, sending a cloud of dust into the air.

"You could use a bath, brother."

Basil nickered softly, his fuzzy white ears pointed toward the turnout. He knew exactly where they were going.

Smiling, Brooks reached for the gate and pushed it open. Basil was a guest favorite at the ranch. He was slow and gentle. Swaybacked enough, that to a tender and chafed butt, he was as comfortable as an old recliner.

Porter had taken the rest of the crew out for a ride along the river, but Owen had stayed behind, admitting at the last minute to a lingering fear of horses. Brooks had convinced him to take Basil for a spin around the arena. At a meandering walk, of course. In Brooks's experience, it was always better to give a reluctant guest another option, rather than let them bow out of an activity all together. People usually felt accomplished after facing a fear, or working through something they didn't think they'd be able to. Brooks was proud that Diamond in the Rough was beginning to build a reputation not just as a fun vacation destination, but also as a therapeutic retreat. A place for folks to reset a bit. To grow and evolve, even if it was only for a few weeks at a time.

He reached up to unbuckle Basil's worn leather halter and watched as the horse made his way over to the apple tree. The branches were hanging over the side of the fence like leafy arms, beckoning him over. He lowered his head to take a nibble, his long white tail swishing at some flies.

"Go easy on those," Brooks said. "You'll get fat."

Basil ignored that and shifted so that his sizeable rear end was facing the man with the dumb advice.

"I see how you are," Brooks muttered. Then shook his head and walked through the gate again, pulling it shut behind him.

He looked toward the house for the third time in as many minutes. Expecting what, he didn't know. For Daisy to come running into his arms?

He'd been trying to avoid thinking of the other night too much. Because in his heart, he knew if he allowed himself to go there, if he let himself think of the sweet memory of her moving underneath him, he might not recover. Ever.

It was just easier this way. To push everything away to a safe distance where it couldn't hurt him. But he'd seen the look in her eyes at dinner last night, and he wondered if she might regret what they'd done. He might be trying to pretend it never happened, but deep down, he'd never regret it. Because he'd been waiting ten long years to touch her again. To hear his name uttered from those full, pink lips.

He rubbed the back of his neck. The truth, giving into her again was also shedding some light on their teenage romance. He'd been blaming Daisy all this time for leaving, for not giving him the chance to come around. It was only now that he'd started wondering if he should blame himself. It was just a glimmer of self-awareness, because let's face it— if losing her was all his fault, he didn't think he could take that, either. But the thought kept gnawing at his belly until he found himself looking over at the house. Again.

He slung the halter and lead rope over his shoulder and walked toward the water pump for a drink but slowed when he saw a small silver car coming down the dusty lane.

Frowning, he pushed his Stetson up on his forehead. It was late in the day, almost suppertime. A strange time for a visitor, especially one in a car he didn't recognize. A car so small that it looked like a bullet, bouncing over the ruts in the road. He could almost hear its suspension groaning from where he stood.

He watched as the car pulled up in front of the house. Something about that made him uneasy. Maybe it was the way the driver had come to such an abrupt stop, the tires skidding in the gravel. Or maybe it was the out of state plates. He ground his teeth together, feeling his jaw tighten like a wire.

The car's driver's side door opened, and a man stepped out. He wore dark sunglasses, his wavy blond hair wild around his face.

Brooks froze. *No way.* No way had Alex O'Brien stepped foot on his ranch. No way in hell did he have the balls to show up here.

The other man swiped his sunglasses off and looked around. Brooks stood there staring. Trying to bring his heartbeat down a notch. But a slow, hot fury was unfurling inside his chest anyway—something so strong, he worried what might happen if he didn't get a handle on it in the next few seconds. All his anger, all his resentment and pain over the last several years, rested with this man in one way or another.

Alex turned and faced him. Recognition must've set in, because he immediately stiffened. Like he was trying to root himself in place. Brooks hadn't seen him since the day he and Daisy had left Marietta, which also happened to be the same day he'd punched him directly in the mouth. Another confrontation that hadn't ended well. He liked to think he'd grown since then, matured like all men should, but he wasn't feeling it at the moment. His hands curled into fists all by themselves.

Alex tucked his sunglasses into his shirt pocket and made a beeline straight for Brooks. Apparently, he wasn't here for Daisy. At least not yet. Which was fine, because there was only so much Brooks could handle at the moment.

He planted his feet apart and slid his hand down the lead rope hanging over his shoulder. The sun was hot on the back of his neck, burning it, but he barely noticed. All he saw right then were those ten years without Daisy. Ten years when she'd been someone else's wife, someone else's lover. She'd given this man a decade of her life. Again, there was that glimmer of self-awareness. If he'd wanted Daisy, he should've fought for her.

But then it was gone. And all he saw was red.

"Brooks?"

Alex's voice had changed. It was low and smooth now, and spoken with the confidence of someone who was used to getting what he wanted.

Brooks nodded, then pulled his hat low. He could smell the other man's cologne on the breeze—something sweet and heavy. Completely out of place on the ranch where the heaviest scent was the cattle, and even they didn't smell that bad, as far as Brooks was concerned.

Alex walked up, stepping carefully over a dried pile of manure. His loafers looked expensive. His slacks and dress shirt looked expensive, too. And hot underneath the late afternoon sun.

"I was worried I might not be able to find you," he said.

"It's been so long. I wasn't even sure you'd still be in Marietta."

Brooks watched him, feeling like a coiled snake.

"So…I take it you're still pissed."

At that, Brooks felt the corners of his mouth twitch. He'd only known the boy. He didn't know the man, but from what he remembered, it was just like him to trivialize what had happened between them to fit his own narrative. Of course, Brooks wasn't sure what that narrative was yet, but now he was getting curious.

"Yeah," he said. "I'm still pissed. Why the hell wouldn't I be?"

"I just thought we could let bygones be bygones. You know. After all this time."

Brooks stared at him.

"Nice place you've got here," Alex said, looking around. "When did you get into the dude ranching business?"

"Cut the shit, O'Brien. What are you doing here?"

Alex's gaze shifted back. The tension between them crackled and sparked. It was a mounting storm, and no amount of small talk was going to make it go away.

"I came out to see Kristen," Alex said slowly. His unruly hair blew about his face, and he ran a hand through it. A wide silver band on his ring finger flashed in the sunlight.

Brooks stared at it. He and Daisy were divorced. Officially. Why would he still be wearing his ring, unless he hadn't quite come to terms with that yet? Brooks felt his chest tighten, realizing this was exactly what he'd been afraid of. Falling for her, only to lose her all over again. When it came to giving her all the things she deserved, he couldn't compete with Alex. He never could.

"And you came to see Daisy," he said evenly.

"Yes. I've been trying to reach her, but I guess she changed her number."

The thought that Daisy might be running away from her life in Boston, just like she'd run away from Marietta, hadn't really occurred to Brooks until right that minute. He'd wanted to believe there was a part of her that was happy to be back, even if he didn't quite trust that she'd stay. But maybe she'd left Alex behind, just like she'd left Brooks. It was a possibility. And his heart beat slow and heavy inside his chest.

"Well," Brooks said, taking off his Stetson to wipe his brow. "She's inside cooking supper."

Alex's mouth curved into a smile. Brooks didn't like it. In fact, he wanted to wipe it right off his face.

"She's cooking for you, huh?" Alex said. "That's what I heard. You know she despises cooking, right?"

He stared at the other man, wondering why he'd never been able to see the undercurrent of cruelty before. Because he'd been a dumb kid, probably. They'd all been dumb kids.

"What's your point?"

"Nothing," Alex said. "Just that she's good at that. Making you believe something when just the opposite is true."

"So, you're speaking from experience?"

Alex shrugged. "I'm here, aren't I?"

"Meaning?"

"Meaning, I've been dancing around what I thought Daisy wanted for years. I thought she wanted to leave here. I thought she wanted to be with me."

Brooks looked down at the worn lead rope in his hand, running his thumb over the threads that were soft as down against his skin. He'd been meaning to get a new one for Basil, but he liked the old one. The old one had memories attached to it.

He looked back up and squinted against the sun that was beginning to make its golden descent into the west—toward Copper Mountain and the jagged Montana landscape where it would sleep. "She did want to leave here. Daisy wasn't going to do anything she didn't want to, O'Brien. Even marrying you."

"Yeah, well." Alex smiled, but there was a bitterness there. "I'm sorry for how all that went down, Brooks."

He'd felt betrayed by Alex, no doubt. But the inconvenient truth was, the guy had been incredibly young. He'd simply seen an opportunity—a beautiful woman whom he'd probably lusted after for a while, and he'd moved on her. Sleezy? Yeah. But the real betrayal, or the real *hurt*, had come from Daisy herself. Brooks had meant what he'd just said. Daisy would've left anyway. Alex, or no. His mother had the same wildness to her, the same desire to run. And she'd left the same broken hearts scattered in her wake, too.

"It was a long time ago," he said.

"It was. I'd do it differently now."

Brooks nodded. "And how's that?" he asked. Not really wanting to know the answer, but knowing it anyway.

"I'd come to you first. I'd tell you how I felt about her. It's what I should've done then. But I wouldn't have just walked away from her, either."

Brooks hadn't walked away. But he'd let her go. He'd definitely let her go.

"I took Daisy for granted," Alex continued, his voice low. "And I think I'm just now seeing that. I think the time away might've helped. Maybe being faced with the rest of my life without her. Things didn't turn out for us the way I was expecting when I was nineteen...the family, the traditional home, all of that never happened. But I can see beyond that now."

"Good for you."

"I never said I wasn't flawed."

Slapping the lead rope methodically against his thigh, Brooks nodded again. "So you want her back, then." It wasn't a question.

"She's my wife."

"She's your ex-wife."

Alex smiled. "I think I was right."

Brooks watched him.

"You want her back, too," he continued. "Tell me I'm

wrong."

A slow heat crept up Brooks's neck. He hadn't admitted as much even to himself over the last few weeks. He sure as shit wasn't going to go there with a man that he'd still like to sucker punch, if he was being honest.

"She made her decision a long time ago," he said evenly.

"She did. And now it's my job to make that decision right."

Alex's gaze grew cool. And he turned to go.

"Wait," Brooks said. "Wait just a damn minute."

The other man stopped in his dusty tracks. He reached into his pocket for his sunglasses and put them on, his mouth settling into a hard line.

Brooks took a few steps forward, careful to keep a safe distance. "Have you stopped to think about *why* she came back to Marietta? Maybe it doesn't have anything to do with you."

"And maybe it doesn't have anything to do with you, either."

"I never said it did. It's pretty clear to me now that she's trying to reconcile what happened with Lou. She's trying to fix something inside her that's been broken for a long time. And maybe she doesn't need you to come waltzing back here to open up those old wounds."

Alex pushed his sunglasses up. They were so dark, Brooks couldn't see his eyes. The intent in them.

"Why don't you let me decide what's best for us, okay?"

Brooks forced a breath. And then another, until he felt the oxygen saturate his lungs, instead of just skimming over them. "All I'm saying, is that she's doing well here. She's healing. If she wants to go back to Boston, great. I wish you both the best. But let her get her feet underneath her first."

Alex put his hands in his khaki pockets. "And would that be for her benefit? Or yours?"

Brooks looked past him. Standing on the front porch in the distance, was Daisy. Her summer dress blew against her legs, her faded apron tied snugly around her waist. She was holding a hand up to shield her eyes from the sun and looking in their direction.

He swallowed hard. It no longer mattered what he thought. Maybe it never did. Daisy would heal in her own time, in her own way.

With one more look at Alex, he grit his teeth. Then touched the brim of his hat and walked away.

Chapter Thirteen

Don't overcrowd the pan.

"WHAT THE..."

Daisy stood on the porch, the wind chimes tinkling delicately beside her. Alex took a step up, but she held up a hand to stop him. She felt ambushed. And, yeah, thanks to Kylee, she knew this had been a possibility, but she never thought he'd actually show up at the ranch, of all places. And he'd been talking to Brooks. Fantastic. What had *that* been about? She could guess well enough, and the knowledge made her stomach turn.

Her ex-husband, the one with the expensive Italian shoes and the sports car that could've funded their non-existent child's first year of college, swiped off his sunglasses and gazed up at her.

"Is that all the welcome I get?"

She glanced over at the car. "You *drove* here?"

"Sure. I like road trips, and it gave me time to think."

"Why?" she asked, looking back at him. "Why did you do this?"

"Because we need to talk."

She laughed. "Alex, we've talked. Remember? We talked and talked, and went around and around, and it never got us anywhere."

"I know. But that was before."

"Before what?"

Leaning toward her, he put a hand on the porch railing. He smelled like a *GQ* ad. His blue eyes sparkled in the late-afternoon light, distinguished wrinkles radiating from their corners. Alex was good-looking, but he knew it, which had always made him seem unapproachable. Even today, Daisy felt a certain amount of intimidation in the way he moved, like he had an important meeting that she was making him late for.

"Before I realized what we had."

Daisy took an instinctive step back. This wasn't supposed to be happening. They were supposed to be amicably divorced. He was supposed to have moved on, and she was supposed to be making her way in Marietta again. He was not supposed to be standing three feet away about to apologize.

"What we had wasn't working," she said.

"Because I hadn't accepted certain things. I feel like I've worked through a lot since you left. I realized I don't need what I thought I did. I miss you."

She watched him carefully. She'd waited for this. For him to say what she'd longed to hear. That she was enough.

Even though she couldn't give him children, and she hadn't settled into the important lifestyle he'd wanted, she was still enough. It had been what she'd wanted to hear from her mother, too. And she never had.

And here Alex was, telling her these things. But now they didn't sound nearly as sweet as she'd imagined. Now, it sounded like he was settling for her. Once upon a time, maybe that would've been enough. Maybe she would've been happy being taken care of and loved just enough to get by. But here, now, standing on the porch of the sprawling old ranch house that had come to mean something to her, the words felt flat.

Even if Alex hadn't thought she was enough, she knew she was. She mattered. She'd been brave enough to come back here, to take this job, to love again. And that was exactly what had happened, wasn't it? She'd fallen in love again. Whether or not Brooks loved her back didn't matter. She was going to feel that love to her bones—the love for him, the love for her mother, the love for her sister, who was about to bring a new life into the world. Daisy had always had love in her life. She just had to come home again to find it.

Taking a deep breath, she took a step down toward Alex. Then another, and another, until she was standing right in front of him. Until she could see the flecks of green in his eyes. A long time ago, she'd thought he would rescue her. Turns out, she was the only one who could do that.

She smiled, but it was small, subdued. "I think what you probably miss is the stability of what we had," she said quietly. "You could always count on it being a certain way, and I understand that, because I felt the same. It grounded me."

He shook his head. "No. That's not it."

"But it is, Alex," she said. "You've always loved the idea of me. And for a long time, I was alright with that. It was enough. But it's not anymore. I deserve more."

He frowned. And it was the first time she'd ever seen that particular expression cross his face. "I do love you."

"In your way, I believe it. But if we ever got back together, you'd be settling for me, and I don't want that."

He watched her, his eyes bright. "You were never my consolation prize, Daisy."

"But I wasn't what you needed. And that's okay. You should be happy. We both should."

"And this is going to make you happy? Working as a short order cook at a dude ranch?"

She squared her shoulders. When she'd come here that very first day, she had no idea what was going to make her happy. She just needed something to be proud of. Something that was *hers*. And somehow, through trial and error, she'd gotten just that. "At the moment?" she said. "Yes."

A silence settled over them, the breeze moving the wind chimes, and making them tinkle and ding. The screen door was open behind Daisy, and Elvira mewed, ready for dinner.

She was always ready for dinner—just one of dozens of little details that Daisy had tucked away these last few weeks. Things that made this place feel more like a home than a business. Dangerous thinking? Probably. But it was becoming harder and harder not to lean into how she felt. She was just so tired of denying it. That didn't mean things would always work out like she wanted in her heart. But she could take away the little bits of joy here and there, and actually make a life out of them. It was a hell of a lot more than a lot of people had. And she was thankful for it.

Alex turned and looked out at the ranch, at the barn in the distance and the river winding so gently next to the pastures. He was still, quiet, his jaw working.

Finally, he pulled in a breath and let it out slowly. "Good God, it's gorgeous out here."

Daisy felt the heaviness in her chest lighten a little. "Yes, it is."

He turned back and settled his gaze on hers. It was frank, no-nonsense. And she braced herself.

"Be honest," he said. "Is Brooks what brought you back here? To Marietta?"

And there it was. The question she must've asked herself a hundred times since showing up at the ranch. Maybe she'd been drawn back to Brooks all along.

She looked down at her clasped hands in front of her belly. "I think…probably. Yes. He was part of it."

"So, what? You want to get back together? With your

high school boyfriend? Actually, never mind. I can see it written all over your face."

"Even if I did want to get back together," she said evenly, "I'll remind you that it's none of your business anymore, remember? You left *me*."

"I know. And that's why I came here. To ask for another chance. But if I'm up against Brooks Cole…" He shook his head. "Well. That's a battle I'm never going to win, is it?"

It was true. And they both knew it. Brooks had always held her heart in his hands. Even now, it was his to do with as he pleased. And the knowledge sent a shiver up her spine. Again, she told herself that she wasn't powerless here. She could choose how much she would let this hurt.

"Right now, Alex," she said, "I'm just going to concentrate on treating myself better. Forgiving myself. In the end, that's why I think I came back. Over everything else."

He nodded slowly, then gave her a smile. One of his most handsome. And she remembered why she'd been charmed by him in the first place. Alex was going to be okay. He was going to find someone else. Someone who'd be able to go toe to toe with him, and who would appreciate all the things that made Alex, Alex. And when he did, she was going to be happy for him.

He reached for her hand and took it in his. His skin felt familiar, comforting. But in a saying goodbye kind of way. They'd grown up together, and then grown apart. In a way, they were closer than ever because of that shared experience.

They were now part of each other's history, for better or worse.

"I guess I never really thought there was much of a chance," he said, his voice low. "But I had to try."

"You don't like giving up."

"No, ma'am."

"What are you going to do now?"

He shrugged. "Go back to Boston. Try and build some kind of long-distance relationship with my sister. Family is important. You taught me that by coming back here."

Her chest warmed. She'd hadn't thought he'd been paying attention. Family was a lesson she was still getting her arms around. It made her happy that he might be following suit, in his own way.

She squeezed his hand. "Let me know when you make it back safe."

He nodded.

"And do me a favor, Alex?"

"Anything."

"Stop by Saint Nicholas sometime? Tell them I said hello."

He smiled. "I should've seen how important the volunteer work was to you. I'm sorry about that."

"I'm sorry about a lot of things, too."

"I still don't get what you see in this place besides the view," he said, looking around again. "But I hope you get everything you want, Daisy. I really do."

He rubbed his thumb over her knuckles, and then let her hand go. And it felt final.

She didn't know if she'd get everything she wanted. But she had to believe she was on the right path. For the first time in a very long time, she was on the right path.

"I hope you do, too," she said.

And meant it.

Chapter Fourteen

Take notes as you go, or you'll forget the things that make a recipe your own.

BROOKS RUBBED THE old cloth over his favorite saddle with a little more force than necessary to make it shine, but what the hell. It was working. The cracked leather absorbed the oil like a sponge, drinking it up after years of hard, everyday use. Brooks couldn't remember the last time he'd done this, taken care of his tack like he should. But he couldn't stomach the thought of going in for dinner tonight, looking at Daisy across the table, and having his heart break all over again.

So, he'd taken the coward's way out and had texted Porter that he had some last-minute chores, making sure to keep it vague so his brother wouldn't catch on. It had worked, and now he had the tack room, and the entire barn to himself so he could think.

Some pigeons cooed in the rafters above, shaking their feathers and sending a few floating down, like snowflakes. He breathed in the musty smell of animal and leather and hay, and tried to clear his mind with its familiarity. The ranch was the most solid thing in his life these days. He knew what to expect from it, and it never surprised him with anything new.

He turned the cloth over in his hand and began working it around the saddle horn until the leather shone in a rich, coffee-colored luster. Rubbing his thumb over it, he thought of Daisy. And how seeing her again had turned his world upside down. Never in a million years would he have thought Alex O'Brien would show up here. That Brooks would have the chance to fight for her like he hadn't as a young man.

Gritting his teeth, he rubbed the cloth over the seat of the saddle and watched it transform before his eyes. All it needed was a little TLC. For someone to see its potential again. He guessed the same could be said of Daisy. She'd come here and transformed herself back into that fiery, independent girl he'd known before. How much of that had to do with him? Had he given her the confidence she'd needed in the beginning? He liked to think he had. But he also remembered wanting to see her fail a little, and he wasn't proud of that. But there were so many emotions, so many feelings unfurling inside of him, that trying to make sense of them all was like trying to rope a single bronc in a stampeding herd of a hundred.

Standing up, he reached for the lightbulb string overhead. A soft, dusky light filled the tack room. Outside, the crickets had begun their evening serenade, a duet alongside the bullfrogs croaking from the dampest parts of the pastures. He couldn't see it from where he stood, but he knew the moon was rising in the east, a beautiful silver charm that would hang over Marietta while she slept.

Beyond the barn's big, open doors, there were footsteps in the gravel. They were soft, measured. Brooks looked at his watch and frowned. It was well past suppertime. The group inside would be working on dessert now, with an eye toward crawling into bed soon. They'd be especially tired with the trail ride. He was pretty sure whoever was on their way to the barn now wasn't on a moonlit stroll.

He waited as the footsteps grew louder, more purposeful, and then muted, as whoever it was stepped inside the barn and onto the soft carpet of hay and packed dirt.

His heart beat steadily inside his chest, as he caught a familiar scent on the soft evening breeze. Daisy's perfume.

"Brooks?"

He folded the cloth slowly, meticulously, and put it back on the shelf alongside the oil. "In here," he answered.

After a second, she appeared in the doorway of the tack room, looking as pretty as ever. She had a simple gray sweater on over her sundress and had it pulled snug around her shoulders. Her hair was up, showing off her long, slender neck. The small diamond studs in her earlobes sparkled underneath the gritty barn lighting, as if they'd been waiting for this moment to fancy the place up.

"Porter said you might be out here."

Brooks stood and lifted the saddle onto a rack next to a row of bridles. "I had some chores to finish up."

"He also said you were probably full of crap about the chores."

He looked over at her. "Oh yeah?"

"He said you were just having a moment and needed some time to yourself."

It figured. Porter knew him almost better than he knew himself. And he'd have heard by now that Alex had made an appearance.

"Is that true?" she asked, her voice low.

Half of him wanted to dodge the question, just to get her to leave him alone. The other half wanted to get into it. All of it, and have it out right here in the middle of the barn. But what would that accomplish? According to her, it would clear the air. And then what? The way Brooks saw it, there was just no path forward that made any sense. He couldn't forgive her yet for leaving and wasn't sure he ever really could. And he sure as hell didn't trust her to stay.

Which led him to the most important question of all. Did he *want* her to stay? He'd built his life on a book of rules he'd written for himself as a teenager. Those rules hadn't changed in all these years. *People leave.* If a heart wanted to wander, it would find a way.

He looked down at the saddle and ran his hand over the smooth, worn leather, the tangy scent of the oil, sharp in his nostrils. Maybe the possibility of her leaving wasn't even the problem. Maybe what he was really afraid of was her staying put. What then? He might just have to throw that book of rules right out the damn window and look inward for once. Focus on his own shortcomings, and why he'd always been so afraid to settle down.

"Brooks."

He glanced over. "Yeah."

"Is that true? Are you out here because you're working? Or are you thinking?"

"I'm working. And thinking."

She took a few steps forward, her arms crossed over her chest. "We missed you at dinner."

He nodded.

"They all leave on Sunday," she continued with a smile. "I've gotten attached."

"Yeah, I know. I'm still not used to that part."

"And we're going to have a dance?" she asked. "On Saturday?"

"That's the plan."

She grazed her bottom lip with her teeth. "That'll be nice. A nice way to say goodbye."

He watched her. Ready to cut to the chase and just get it over with. "Why did you come out here, Daisy? And don't tell me it was because you missed me."

"I did miss you."

"Right."

"Why is that so hard for you to believe?"

He shrugged, picking a bridle off one of the hooks and brushing some grass off the bit before putting it back again. "Maybe because today I had a nice chat with your ex, and you might be worried that I'm pissed."

Her expression fell. "Alright. I'm a little worried, yes."

"Well, you don't have to worry. I'm fine."

"You don't look fine."

He ran a hand through his hair, well aware that his face was probably red, and getting redder by the second.

Reaching up, he yanked on the lightbulb string, and the tack room went gray. He brushed past Daisy and into the barn where a few of the horses were rustling the hay in their stalls. Friday, all the animals would be turned out into the pastures, and a temporary stage would be brought in for the live band. Little white lights would be strung up everywhere, and there would be strawberry lemonade and a tower of chocolates from Copper Mountain Chocolate Shop on a table by the doors. She was right—it would be a nice good-bye. But the problem with goodbyes was that Brooks had said too many of them to last a lifetime.

He heard her follow him out. The natural light in the barn was fading fast, but he didn't bother switching on the overheads. He wasn't going to stay anyway. He'd changed his mind about wanting to get into it. Now, he just wanted as far away from her and the way she was making him feel, as possible. Like his heart was going to come off its rusty hinges and fall all the way apart.

"Brooks," she said. "Wait. Where are you going?"

"Inside," he said over his shoulder. "I'm beat."

"So, we're not going to talk about this?"

"Talk about what?"

"You know what. Will you just stop for a minute?"

Letting out a breath, he slowed his steps, then turned to face her. It was hard not to be swayed by how she looked—flushed and healthy from the last few weeks in the sun. Big brown eyes, lined with the darkest, thickest lashes he thought he'd ever seen. Hair the color of summer wheat, hanging in delicate strands around her face. Daisy had aged well. The years had been good to her, and the beginnings of the laugh lines around her eyes that others might see as imperfections, only made her more attractive to him. She was older, wiser. She'd come into her own since she'd been gone, she really had.

"What is it, Daisy?" he asked, his voice low. "What do you want to talk about?"

She dropped her hands to her sides, and the thin cardigan fell open, sliding off one smooth, brown shoulder. "I had no idea Alex was going to show up here like that. I'm sorry."

"Nothing to be sorry about."

"So you're not upset."

"Nope."

"What did he say?"

Brooks touched one ear to his shoulder until his neck

popped. "Just made his intentions clear. You know. In case I had a thing for you."

She frowned, some of the color going out of her cheeks. The light was crap, but he could see that part clear enough. "Oh. And what did you say?"

"I told him I thought you were happy here. And that he should leave you alone to be happy. And that there was nothing going on between us."

"Well…" She bit her lip for a second before going on. "That's partly true."

"What part?"

"The happy part. The part where he should give me space. But there's definitely something going on between us."

Brooks put his hands in his pockets, feeling his plaid shirt stretch over his shoulders. Every muscle in his body felt bunched, tight. Like he wanted to climb right out of his skin. Lying about how he felt was getting practically impossible. But it looked like he was going to try and go to his grave lying to Daisy.

"We slept together," he said. "I blame that nightgown of yours." That part was meant to lighten the mood, but there was more than an element of truth to it. He cleared his throat and plowed on. "But as far as what happens now, we both knew we'd end up right back where we started. And I take full responsibility for that."

She glared at him. "You don't get to do that."

"Do what?"

"That, *aww shucks, ma'am, I messed up all on my own,* crap. I made a choice, too. And it wasn't my nightgown, or the time of night, or how much wine I had with dinner. I knew exactly what I was doing, so just stop trying to take all the credit here."

He felt his mouth harden. "People don't tell me what to do, Daisy," he said, making sure to keep his voice flat. Emotionless. He was being a dick, but he wasn't prepared to turn back now. She was absolutely right, and his heart, his pride was on the line.

"Oh, I know. You're used to doing exactly what you want. Without considering the consequences."

"That's not true. And it's not fair."

"Might not be true 100 percent of the time, but in my experience, it's true plenty."

"I considered the consequences with us."

"But are you considering them now? With this walking away garbage?"

"We both decided—"

She held up a hand. "I know what we both decided, blah, blah, blah. Don't you see what's happened here? I'm falling back in love with you. It doesn't matter what I decided I didn't *want* to happen. It *did* happen, and now we need to talk about this. To face it. Together."

"Nope." He turned on his heel and headed for the barn doors and the dusky evening beyond. "No way," he said over his shoulder. "I know where this is going, and we already did it once. It didn't work, remember?"

She hustled after him. "*Ten* years ago, Brooks. And we never solved anything back then. We only made it worse by walking away."

At that, he stopped and whipped around. "You were the one who walked away, baby. I didn't go anywhere."

She narrowed her beautiful eyes, looking like she wanted to stick a knife neatly between his ribs. "I know. You keep reminding me over and over again."

"Somebody's got to remind you."

"Why? In case I forget? I'm never going to forget, Brooks. I'm going to feel the guilt from leaving my entire life. But I'm choosing to move past it. People change. I've changed."

At that, he wanted to grab her by the shoulders. To lean down and crush his mouth to hers. Make her *want* to stay. But he didn't because all he could picture was her driving away that day. With another man, toward another life.

She stepped slowly forward, until she was close enough to touch, and tipped her head back to look up at him. "This has nothing to do with wanting to get back together," she said. "This has to do with me accepting things I know are fact and finding a way to live with them."

He swallowed hard—the urge to touch her so strong, that the tips of his fingers tingled with it. "And those facts? What are those?"

"I left. Fact. That was on me. And if I'd stayed, who knows what would've happened with us. Because, you're right. You might've come around if I'd given you time."

He watched her.

"But you might not have, either," she said. "You were pretty convincing when you told me you didn't need anyone. The question is, have *you* changed, Brooks?"

He hadn't. He knew he hadn't, not where it really counted. Sure, he'd grown up; he understood things now that he hadn't before. He got that his mother's abandonment had happened at a critical point in his adolescence and had created a wound that might never fully heal. He understood that falling in love with Daisy and having her leave, too, only served to make that wound bigger, more painful. He got all that. With his brain, he got it. But it was his heart that was having the hardest time coming to terms with it. And accepting that the woman standing before him now wasn't the same person who'd left before. She'd said it herself. She'd changed. So why couldn't he accept that and finally take a chance with someone again?

"You know the answer to that," he said, his voice low.

"You still blame me."

"I blame us both."

She was quiet then, and so was he. The crickets chirped outside the barn and one of the horses nickered softly. It would've been a peaceful night, a beautiful night, if it wasn't for that old, familiar bitterness settling between them.

She pulled her sweater tight again, as if warming herself against his chill. "I just wanted to tell you that I'm sorry Alex came here. And that he and I were over a long time ago. Probably the second we left Marietta, to tell you the truth."

He nodded. Her lips glistened under the moonlight coming in through the barn doors. Her dark eyes reflected it and sparkled like onyx.

"And I just wanted to say…" Her voice was soft. So soft, that he knew she was trying not to cry. "That I love you."

He stood there looking down at her as the nighttime sounds of the ranch floated in on the cool breeze. Then, he leaned close, until he could smell the perfume on her skin. Until he could feel the warmth of her body next to his. Until all the memories of the last decade were gone, and it was just the two of them, standing in an old barn, about to kiss.

I love you, too, he wanted to say.

Instead, he pressed his lips to hers. She stood there for a minute, stiff. Maybe expecting an answer. Some kind of verbal response. But honestly, at the moment, this was the best he could do.

After a second, she relaxed into him, standing on her tip-toes and wrapping her arms around his neck. He took that as an invitation, and urged her lips open with his tongue. They were soft and smooth as silk and tasted like berries warmed in the sun. She made a little sound in the back of her throat as he wrapped an arm around her waist, bringing her closer. Her breasts were warm and giving against his chest, and he could feel her hardened nipples through his shirt.

He hadn't planned on this. When he'd looked up to see her in the tack room a few minutes ago, he'd planned on getting up and walking out. But Daisy had a way of pulling him back in. Just when he thought he had control of his feelings for her, just when he thought he was the one driving this, she reminded him that wasn't the case. Never had been.

Gently, he took her by the wrists, and broke the kiss. The barn was so dark now, that it would be easy to tell himself she didn't look hurt by that. That the tilt of her head and the curve of her shoulders wasn't the dawning of a cold realization for her. But he knew better. He was pushing her away. Physically, now, as well as emotionally.

She stood there looking up at him. Watching, waiting. He owed her a response, something to solidify where this was going between them. Or where it wasn't going. He knew it wasn't fair to keep her hanging after she'd just said she loved him. He knew this. Still, he couldn't find the words that would solidify a damn thing.

He brushed her hair away from her face, moving his thumb over her cheekbone. Her skin was as soft as a rose petal underneath his, and he found himself savoring the moment. He wanted to touch her again and again and again. In fact, he never wanted to stop touching her. But she wasn't his. She wasn't anyone's. She'd come home again, but she had a restless spirit.

"You're not going to want to be a cook here forever, Daisy," he said quietly. "And then what?"

She stepped forward, but he leaned away.

"No. Just let me say this, okay?"

She lifted her chin and took a visible breath. "Okay."

"You're going to grow and heal," he said. "And you'll be able to do that in Marietta, because it's a safe place and people care about you here…"

Her eyes filled with tears.

He let his gaze fall to her mouth, because if he looked too long in those eyes, he wouldn't be able to say this, and he needed to.

"I know you're looking for a certain kind of love, Daisy. You've been looking for it your entire life. Your dad left. Lou was too damaged to be able to give you what you needed. And then I let you down, too."

The tears hovered on her bottom lids for a minute, then spilled down her cheeks in two glistening tracks.

"It wasn't because I didn't love you," he said. "I think it was because I loved you too much. I couldn't stand the thought of starting a life with you, of starting a family with you, and then losing you."

She licked the tears from her lips, then gave him a small, sad smile. "Alex and I could never have a family. See? You didn't have to worry."

He frowned down at her. "You actually think you're broken, don't you? Somehow, you've thought that this whole time."

She let out a little sob then, and he reached for her, but this time she was the one to lean away.

She wiped her eyes with the backs of her knuckles and straightened her shoulders. "I'm sorry. I didn't want to do this. I wanted to be the strong one and show you how independent I am now." She laughed. "Guess that flew right out the window, huh?"

"You've always been strong, Daisy."

Somewhere in the rafters above, the pigeons were settling in for the night, cooing softly to each other. In the distance, there was the sound of the occasional truck lumbering past on the highway, gearing down for the long climb up the mountain.

Right then, Brooks didn't give a shit if she did end up leaving. He didn't care that Alex had tracked her down and had probably planted some kind of seed in her heart. And he didn't care that holding her now would make it harder in the long run. He simply reached for her and pulled her close.

As she rested her cheek against his chest, he wondered if he'd done this ten years ago, if things might've been different for them. If his dad had simply pulled his mother close, maybe she would've seen something worth saving.

Right then, he found that it didn't matter. Nothing mattered but the feel of her warm, even breaths through his shirt.

Chapter Fifteen

Don't make meringue on a rainy day! The humidity will keep it from setting like it should, and nobody wants goopy meringue.

D AISY LEANED DOWN to retrieve the pie, the hot air from the oven slamming her directly in the face. She blew on a loose strand of hair and straightened, frowning at the pie like it had personally disappointed her. Which, she guessed it had.

She set it on the cooling rack and closed the oven door with her hip. She was never going to win any contest with pastries like this. It looked like a high school pottery project, its crust drooping dejectedly at one end.

Contest... It was a crazy idea. But over the last few days, ever since Alex had shown up, she hadn't been able to get it out of her head. Not just any contest, but *the* contest. The Marietta pie baking contest that her mother had entered, and won, nearly every year of her adult life.

Taking off her oven mitts, Daisy leaned against the counter. Maybe this was a mid-life crisis. She'd heard of them going down like this, where someone left for the grocery store, and came home driving a cherry-red Corvette. But the thing was, it didn't *feel* like a crisis. It felt more like an awakening of sorts. The perfect way to honor her mother in the most tangible way. And to embark on a new adventure of her own.

Sometimes that was easier said than done.

She stared down at the sad-looking pie with the runny meringue and felt her resolve waver. Brooks was right to question her. He'd always been able to see into the deepest parts of her. Even now, even after being home for weeks, and experiencing all the good things that had come with it, she sometimes had thoughts of leaving. They were only fleeting thoughts, nothing that stuck, but they were there. Because leaving was always easier, wasn't it? Easier than learning how to support herself through a job she didn't know the first thing about. Easier than putting back together a relationship with her sister, that she'd thought was beyond repair. And easier than getting her heart broken by Brooks. Not that he meant to break her heart, but he did, just the same.

She touched the crumbling crust of the pie tenderly. It might not be perfect, but her mom would've found a way to salvage it. She would have served it with extra ice cream to hide the flaws.

"Knock, knock."

Daisy looked up to see Lily standing in the archway of the kitchen, looking adorable, and extra pregnant in a pair of overalls with a soft pink T-shirt underneath.

"Hey!" Grinning, she pulled her baby sister into a hug. "What are you doing here?"

"Oh, I was on my way back from getting Jack some chocolate chip cookies from this place he loves in Bozeman. I'm sending him a care package tomorrow."

Daisy rubbed Lily's shoulder. She was looking forward to meeting her brother-in-law. There was so much she didn't know about him. The fact that he liked chocolate chip cookies should've been a small revelation, but at the moment, it seemed like a big one.

"Anyway," Lily went on, "the Jeep was overheating a little. So I thought I'd stop and let it cool off, and see how you were doing. I heard Alex was back."

"You heard about that, huh?"

"The whole town's heard about it. I guess he made an evening of it at Grey's last night. He and Kylee Turner."

"Good Lord. Why am I not surprised?"

Lily waddled over to a stool and climbed up with a grunt. "She has a way of homing in on other people's men," she said, rubbing her belly. "I think she can sniff out the ones who aren't available."

"Well, he's definitely available, so she can home in all she wants."

Lily looked down at her stomach for a second, plucking a piece of lint off her overalls. "She was telling everyone who would listen that you won't stay. That you think you're too good for Marietta now."

"Lily…you can't pay any attention to that stuff."

"I want to punch her in the face."

Daisy tried not to laugh. It was hard picturing Lily tangling with anyone, but especially now that she was round as a potato bug. "Lily…"

"Well, I do. Where does she get off talking about you like that?"

Daisy walked over to the fridge and pulled out the pitcher of lemonade, then got a couple of cups from the cupboard. "I know you hate to think about it like this," she said, pouring them both a glass, "but you've got to cut her some slack. I didn't exactly leave on great terms, remember."

She handed Lily her lemonade, who took a few long swallows, before setting the glass down on the counter. "I just worry. That's all."

Daisy pulled out a stool and sat next to her. "About?"

"About all the talk getting to you…"

Her sister let her voice trail off, and right then, she looked like a teenager again. So sweet in her overalls, her summer freckles scattered haphazardly across her cheeks.

Daisy reached for her hand and squeezed it. "I know. But I'm not going anywhere this time. I promise."

Lily smiled, her cheeks coloring. "I guess I just like having you back. It's nice. It's nice knowing the baby is going to have her auntie here."

At that, Daisy's heart swelled. There had been a point

not too long ago when she'd resigned herself to the fact that she'd never change a diaper, or sing anyone to sleep, or wash a sticky pair of hands before dinner. She'd told herself that she was okay with it, that not everyone was meant to be a mom. But the longing had stayed put, deep down inside. Sometimes she'd picture what a family with Brooks would look like, before she caught herself and slapped her hand. *Stop. He's not yours. That life isn't yours...*

But now, she saw the miracle, the blessing in being able to be a part of her niece's life. It was a gift that she would always be grateful for.

"Hey," she said, wanting to change the subject before she started to cry. "I made a pie."

Lily glanced over at the cooling rack. "I see that. And it smells *so* good."

"Well, it looks a little funny, but Mama always said it's the taste that really counts."

"She did say that, didn't she? For someone who was such a perfectionist, she could be awfully forgiving when she wanted to be."

Lily looked up at her, and Daisy gazed back. They both realized what she'd said at the same moment. *Forgiving...*

Lily touched her knee. "Hey."

Daisy felt the tears coming anyway. She blinked them away, but they were insistent. It was like her body yearned for the release.

"She loved you, Daisy," Lily said. "If she'd had more

time, it would've been different."

She nodded. It was true. She knew it in her bones. She knew it, because eventually Daisy would've come home. She would've made it right, eventually. But the biggest lesson she'd taken away from all this, was that life was finite. There wasn't always time to do with what you pleased. Like the cooking, she knew she had to make use of what she was given now. Today. And be thankful for it.

Elvira sauntered in and wrapped herself around Lily's stool. Her sister looked down at the cat, obviously wanting to reach down to pet her, but her stomach wouldn't allow it.

"She's so cute!"

"She's getting fat," Daisy said. "She eats bacon for breakfast."

"I refuse to hold that against her. And this is Brooks's cat?"

"Yup."

Lily looked back up, her eyes twinkling. "Is this the same Brooks who always told us he'd never have pets in his house?"

"The one and only."

"Seems like somebody's turned into a big softie."

Daisy's heart squeezed, and she had to remind it to stay in its lane. Dumb heart. "Brooks wants what he wants. Or doesn't want what he doesn't want, I guess."

"He used to be harder around the edges. I'm just saying...the way he looks at you..."

It was the same thing Eddie had said. And maybe Brooks did have a way of looking at her. But what everyone else was missing, were the conversations that had happened between the two of them these last few weeks. If Brooks wanted more, he'd let her know. And so far, there wasn't anything forth-coming in that department.

"*Ohh.*" Lily winced and grabbed her belly.

Daisy leaned forward. "What is it, Lil?"

"Nothing. Probably just Braxton Hicks. I've been getting them."

Frowning, she watched her sister like she was about to pop. Which, she absolutely could. Only a few more weeks to go. And then, baby powder, and soft skin, and sleepless nights, and bedtime stories. So many things to look forward to. So many things to cherish.

Lily blew out a long breath. "Can you believe I'm about to be a mom?"

"Honestly, I still see you as a toddler. My baby sister. But you're going to be the best mom, Lily. The very best."

"I don't know. Sometimes I worry. What if I yell too much, like Mama did? Or what if I don't yell enough? What if I can't bond with the baby? Mama told me once that she didn't bond with us right away…"

Her sister looked genuinely scared right then, and Daisy felt that fear acutely. She knew exactly how she felt, because when she and Alex had been trying for a baby, she'd won-dered the same. Sometimes, she'd woken up in the middle of the night, going over and over it. The what ifs. All the things that could go wrong, all the ways she could fail and repeat history. In the end though, she'd decided to trust herself with wanting motherhood. It was a leap of faith, and in her eyes, one worth taking.

"Daisy…" Lily sat forward. "Mama told me a few things that I don't think you ever knew. Things that she struggled with her whole life."

Daisy's heartbeat slowed. She could feel it thumping like something heavy and tired behind her breastbone. Her mother hadn't confided anything to her over the years. Of course, she wouldn't have. They'd barely spoken.

"She lost two babies," Lily said, her voice low. "Did you know that?"

Daisy watched her sister. The clock above the oven ticked the seconds off dutifully and was the only thing she was aware of, besides the blood rushing in her ears.

Slowly, she shook her head, then licked her lips, surprised to find that her tongue worked at all. "No," she managed. "I didn't know that."

"She told me right before she died. I don't know that she'd ever talked about it with anyone before."

Daisy's mom had always been something of a mystery to her. But this was an important puzzle piece, slipping quietly into place. Lou Hudson wouldn't have talked to anyone, because there hadn't been anyone to talk to. Her mother had died. The father of her kids had walked out on her. And then she'd pushed her kids away, too.

"There were two babies after you and me," Lily said. "She couldn't carry them to term, and I guess Daddy blamed her. He was awful. And then he took off and left her with two toddlers. And the rest is history."

The rest is history... Daisy looked out the kitchen window to where the big cottonwood shivered in the breeze. She wondered if knowing this as a child would have changed anything between her and her mother. She had to believe it would have. She might not have understood her mom's pain, but she would've been sensitive to it. She would've at least known the reason behind her bitterness. And maybe she would've been able to look beyond the wall between them and seen something on the other side.

She had to swallow twice to get the lump in her throat to go down. It settled in her chest like a stone, but at least she felt like she could breathe again.

Looking back at Lily, she gave her a small smile. "Thank you for telling me," she said. "I'm glad to know."

"I wasn't sure if you'd want to. I know you and Alex had your own issues with having a family. I didn't want to make you sad."

Daisy reached for her little sister's hand and ran her thumb over her simple gold wedding band. "We struggled, that's true," she said. "But family is what you make it, not what you're given. If Mama taught me anything, if she's *still* teaching me anything, it's not to dwell on the past. And I'm happy now, Lily. I really, truly am."

Lily leaned forward for a hug. Her belly was so big, it was hard to get close, but they clung to each other anyway.

Finally pulling away, Daisy wiped her eyes. "Can you stay for lunch? Porter is out with the group at the lake, and Brooks is getting the barn ready for this weekend. So it'd just be us girls."

"Oh, I'd love that," Lily said, "but I have so much to do. The nursery still isn't ready and there's tons of laundry."

"I'll come over tonight and help. You can put your feet up and relax. Soak in some you time before this little munchkin gets here."

"Well, I've got vanilla ice cream in the freezer," Lily said. "You can bring the pie?"

"It's a date."

Lily eased herself off the stool. "I should at least start on that laundry, though. The burp rags alone are going to take all afternoon."

Daisy took her by the elbow when she swayed on her feet. "Are you okay?"

"I'm good. Just tired."

"Listen," she said, walking her out of the kitchen and toward the front door. "I'm going to call Charlie and ask if she can come help with the meals tomorrow. She's so sweet, she's always offering. I think it's time to take her up on it. I'll spend the day at your place getting everything squared away, okay? You're doing too much."

Lily grabbed her purse by the door as Elvira rubbed insistently against her swollen ankles.

Daisy picked the cat up and plopped her on the couch. "You're a tripping hazard for pregnant people."

"I don't think she cares," Lily said. "I think she's asking for bacon."

"She's got a one-track mind."

"But bacon."

Daisy smiled. "But bacon."

They headed out onto the porch and down the steps, the late morning sunshine warm on their faces. A couple of hummingbirds hovered at the feeder. Their little wings thrummed through the air, and Elvira chirped at them from behind the screen door.

Lily stepped onto the gravel. Then froze and grabbed her stomach.

"Daisy," she said. "I think my water just broke."

Chapter Sixteen

If you're hosting a dinner party, just assume everyone will show up early.

B ROOKS ADJUSTED THE string of lights over one shoulder, then hauled the old ladder over the other. The barn didn't need much to make it festive. Just the lights, a stage, some music, and good food.

His dad would take care of the music on Saturday. Daisy would take care of the food. Together, they were a force to be reckoned with. Two people who'd come back into his life like storm clouds in the spring.

Carrying the ladder over to the stalls, he looked up at the hooks with a critical eye, then set the ladder down as Basil stuck his nose over his gate and nickered.

"Don't have anything for you today, buddy. Besides, you're getting as big as a damn house."

The horse watched him, fuzzy ears pricked. He was used to getting exactly what he wanted, simply by looking cute.

Brooks smiled and reached over to pat his spotted neck. "Tough love. That's what this is. You'll thank me later."

Basil nudged his hand, then sighed and gave up, turning to nose through the straw in the corner.

"Brooks!"

He looked over to see Daisy running into the barn.

"Whoa, whoa. Don't trip over those lights."

She stopped in front of him and put her hands on her knees. "Lily," she panted. "Lily's here, and her water broke, and the Jeep won't start…"

He patted her back. "Daisy. Just breathe, okay?"

She nodded but looked close to passing out.

"She's having a baby," he said. "This happens every day. She's gonna be fine."

Nodding again, she gazed up at him.

"*Deep* breaths," he said.

She pulled in a breath and held it for a few seconds, before letting it out her puffed cheeks. Her hands were still planted on her knees, but she seemed steadier now.

"You good?"

"I think so." Straightening, she grabbed his arm. "I'm going to be an auntie."

"I know. I know you are, baby. And you're gonna be a great one."

She stared at him, her eyes big and dark. And then she smiled.

"Where is she?" he asked.

"On the porch. She just had a really strong contraction. They seem to be coming pretty fast. I thought first-time babies took forever."

"Not necessarily." He'd spent enough time on the ranch to know that wasn't always the case. Far from it. Mother Nature always had a few surprises up her sleeve.

"Let me get my keys," he said, "and I'll pull the truck around."

She stood on her tiptoes and planted a warm, wet kiss on his lips.

"What's that for?"

"For being here when I need you. For calming me down. For looking so good in those jeans."

She smiled as she said this, looking impish and utterly charming. She didn't wait for him to respond. Just turned and jogged back toward the house.

He didn't have time to watch her go like he normally would've. Watching Daisy go wasn't the worst thing in the world. Instead, he headed for the tack room and grabbed his keys off the hook.

His truck was stifling. He started it and rolled down the windows to get the air circulating before the air conditioner took over. Daisy and Lily were sitting on the porch steps when he pulled up, dust billowing around the truck. He hopped out, came around and clapped his hands.

"Ready to get this party started, Mama?"

Lily stared up at him as another contraction took hold. Her entire face crumpled.

Daisy looked worried and rubbed her little sister's back.

After it passed, Brooks bent to one knee. "You got this, honey," he said. "I know Jack isn't here right now, but we are, and we're going to take good care of you, okay?"

Lily's eyes filled with tears. "It hurts. I'm scared."

"I know you are, but you're a rock star. And when it's all said and done, you're going to have the most beautiful little girl. When her daddy gets home, he'll be so proud of you both."

The tears spilled over her cheeks and dripped onto her T-shirt.

"Can you get into the truck, Lil?" Daisy asked.

She nodded, and Brooks and Daisy each grabbed an arm to help her up. She frowned. "My pants are wet. Your truck…"

"Don't worry about that," Brooks said. "We just need to get you to the hospital."

"For drugs," she said.

"For drugs." He caught Daisy's eye and she smiled back. Maybe it was the moment. Maybe it was how vulnerable she looked—like a first-time mother herself. But he felt a rush of love for her right then that nearly stole the air from his lungs. He wanted to wrap her in his arms and hold her close. Keep her safe from everything that could hurt her. She deserved all the happiness that life could throw her way. Happiness and love that she'd missed out on as a kid.

For the first time, he wondered about trying to give it to her himself, and the thought pierced his heart like a well-aimed arrow. Did he deserve another chance? And more importantly, would he be able to deliver?

He helped Lily into the back seat of the truck and watched as Daisy settled herself beside her. She reached over her sister's belly and pulled the seat belt across. He noticed her hands were shaking. *Lovely Daisy.* He knew what this moment meant to her. She'd broken something, and now she was trying her damnedest to fix it. She wanted her sister to know that she was someone she could count on. They were orphans now, had no family except for each other and Jack, and watching her navigate this experience was doing something to him. Doing something to his heart.

He came around and climbed in the truck. Then put it into gear and peeled out of the gravel drive. In the distance, he could see Clifford running up ahead. A sign that Porter and the rest of the group weren't far behind. The hot midday sun shone through the windshield in bright shards of gold, forcing him to pull the visor down and squint at the road ahead.

Behind him in the back seat, Lily was deep breathing. Daisy was breathing with her, timing the contractions, which seemed strong, and closer together than he would've liked for the hospital being as far away as it was.

"*Oooohh!*" Lily groaned. "It *hurts.* Why don't they tell you it's going to hurt this bad?"

Daisy caught his eye in the rearview mirror. Her brows were furrowed, and her forehead was damp with sweat.

He winked at her, wishing he could pull her close and promise that everything was going to be okay. But the truth was, he couldn't promise anything. He'd experienced enough of life's uncertainty up to this point, that he could only hope.

Hope and pray that it would all work out the way it was supposed to.

BROOKS LEANED AGAINST the wide ledge of the windowsill, looking down at the parking lot of Marietta General. It was nice and cool in here, so he wasn't sweaty anymore, but he still smelled faintly of horse. Which he guessed was okay. The little hospital was no stranger to cowboys walking through its doors, or more often *limping* through its doors. Still, he wished he'd thought to grab a clean shirt before leaving the house.

He glanced up at the clock. The last time Daisy had poked her head out of Lily's room had been an hour ago. Things were progressing, but Lily had been laboring all afternoon, and she was tired. Daisy had looked tired, too. Even the nurses filtering in and out of the room seemed weary and drawn.

Shoving a hand through his hair, he pulled his phone from his back pocket. He'd been texting Jack—trying to relay information when he got it, in a way that wouldn't worry the poor guy to death. But it was obvious he was going out of his mind with it anyway. Brooks couldn't imagine being in another country when his wife went into labor. It was a heavy sacrifice, and he knew when he met Jack in person, he was going to like him.

No word yet, he typed out, *but I'll let you know asap.*

Jack texted back immediately. *Thanks, man.*

A few nurses rushed past, holding onto their stethoscopes to keep them from flapping around their ears. Brooks felt his stomach sink when they pushed open the door to Lily's room. He stood there watching, his pulse thumping in his neck. From down the hall, a doctor came running, then pushed Lily's door open, too. It closed in a soft swoosh, but Brooks had seen enough—the doctors, at least two, and several nurses in colorful scrubs crowding around Lily's bed.

He took a few steps toward her room but knew there was nothing he could do. Just stand outside and wait like a devoted animal. He thought of Jack, thousands of miles away, waiting, too. Hoping for a healthy wife and baby. Hoping nothing would go wrong.

Brooks wasn't much of a praying man, hadn't been for quite some time. When his mother had left, he'd talked to God, but there'd never been an answer. At least not one he'd been able to decipher. When Daisy had married Alex, he'd been so angry, he'd walked away from God altogether. But here, now, he found himself sinking down into one of the plastic waiting room chairs and clasping his hands together. He had no idea what to say but figured the words didn't matter anyway. It was the intention that mattered. The opening of his heart, where it hadn't been open in a very long time.

He looked down at his lap for a second before closing his eyes. The sounds of the hospital carried on around him—the doctors being paged overhead, the gurneys being pushed by, the television in the waiting room tuned on to *The Price is Right!*

But all he was aware of at the moment was the yearning inside him that had grown into an undeniable ache over these last few weeks. But yearning for what? Daisy? It would be easy to assume that, and just leave it there. But really, he knew it was more. It was a yearning for deeper relationships in his life. For peace and stability. For love.

Brooks knew he was now at a crossroads. Which way to go? The route that had proved safe all this time? Or the road at the end of which, Daisy was waiting?

The door to Lily's room opened, and a team of doctors and nurses wheeled her bed out. Standing, he watched as they rushed her down the hall, speaking to each other in low tones. Daisy appeared and stumbled toward him.

He crossed the waiting room and took her gently by the shoulders.

"What happened?"

"I'm not sure. Things were going okay. And then they weren't. The baby's heart rate dropped...something about the umbilical cord. And then Lily's heart rate dropped, and they said they needed to do an emergency C-section." She snapped her fingers. "Just like that."

He pulled her into his arms and held her against his chest. She sagged into him, exhausted. Physically and emotionally.

"I'm so scared, Brooks. What if something happens?"

"It's not going to."

"But what if it does?"

He pushed her away enough to look down into her face, now wet with tears. "It's going to be okay. This hospital has the best doctors around. They're not going to let anything happen to her."

"My mom lost two babies," she said quietly. "Lily just told me today. I never knew."

He nodded. He hadn't known her mother well. Lou Hudson hadn't exactly been the most approachable woman, but this small glimpse into her life humanized her. She'd had it hard. Of course, he'd been young and stupid back then. Rarely stopping to consider anyone else's suffering but his own. There was a sudden rush of guilt for that. Of wishing he could go back and look at her through kinder eyes.

Daisy wiped her cheeks. "It still happens," she said. "Moms still lose babies. We still lose moms…"

"We're not going to lose anyone," Brooks said.

She seemed to consider this, looking out the window to the bright blue sky and the mountains in the distance. There was a lull in the hospital activity around them, even the

TVgoing temporarily quiet during a commercial break. Daisy felt warm and supple against his body, fitting there like an extension of himself. He'd forgotten how well they fit together. How easy it was to be with her.

"It's taken me so long to figure things out," she said, her voice hoarse. "With Mama, with Lily. With you…"

His gaze slipped down to the hollow of her throat. How many times had he kissed that exact spot? How many times had he claimed it for his own? But that was the thing he'd been missing as a young man, which seemed so painfully obvious now. Daisy wasn't anyone's to claim. She was her own woman. She'd left, had found her way back again, had grown and changed. Now, he just needed to figure out where he fit in all that. And how far he was willing to go to find out.

"It's taken so long," she continued. "But I'm happy again. I'm happy with what I've been given. If you and I aren't meant for more, that's okay, because I have you in my life. And I'll take it." She smiled. "If I never get to be a mom, that's okay too, because I'll have Lily and the baby. And I think I've finally found some peace with my mom. I think I know her now. And that's such a gift, Brooks. I can't even tell you…"

He didn't doubt a word of it. Someday, he hoped to come to that place with his own mother. *Maybe someday…*

"But I can't lose anyone else," she said, her voice catching. "I won't."

At that, he pulled her close again, and she lay her cheek against his chest. Her hair smelled like shampoo, something fruity and sweet. It smelled like summer, like home. Her heart beat in time with his, and the cadence lulled him into a place where questions couldn't follow. Right then, they were one.

And he'd take all of that he could get.

Chapter Seventeen

Use honey instead of sugar for the sweetest muffins.

D AISY LOOKED DOWN at the sleeping baby in her arms, suddenly worried she'd forget the details of the moment. She thought of the sticky notes in her mother's cookbook, faded and dog-eared, sticking out of the pages like a weary paper rainbow. All taking note of the little things that were closest to Lou Hudson's heart. All there so she wouldn't forget.

Daisy started a list in her mind... *Heart-shaped lips, the bottom one bigger than the top. The tiniest hint of a cleft chin— a dimple that looks like an angel pressed her finger there. The baby smell...oh the baby smell. The weight of her in my arms...*

She glanced over at Lily, sleeping soundly in her bed. She looked comfortable, leaning back against two fluffy pillows, and draped with a colorful quilt that Brooks had brought from the ranch.

Lily had finally grown still, the excitement and joy of the day taking a back seat to the exhaustion of giving birth. The baby was healthy—a beautiful little girl that her parents had named Clara Lou after her grandmothers. And Lily was healthy, too. She'd lost some blood and would be in the hospital for a few days, but when she got home, Daisy would be there to take care of her. To take care of them both.

As far as the ranch went, Charlie had healed enough from her surgery to offer to take over for a bit, something that Daisy would forever be grateful for. So the next few weeks were going to be spent acclimating this new little family to their routine, to their home, to Marietta in all its warmth and beauty.

Breathing in Clara's newborn scent, Daisy walked over to the window and looked out at the town below. She rocked back and forth, cradling the bundle in her arms. Every now and then, the baby would make a gurgly sound, or a tiny bubble would pop on her cherub lips. Her eyelashes lay long and dark against her rosy cheeks, and were so perfect, Daisy thought she might cry because of it.

Leaning down, she kissed the little girl's temple, then smoothed her fine, honey-colored hair to one side of her forehead. She had a lot of hair. Lily said Jack had a lot of hair when he was a baby. Maybe she got it from her daddy.

"I'm so happy I get to be your auntie," she whispered.

The baby sighed as if in gentle agreement.

"I don't ever want you to run away from anything, okay?" Daisy continued, her voice so soft, it barely registered in her own ears. "You run toward things. Even if they scare you."

The baby's eyelids moved. Maybe she was dreaming. Maybe she'd carried a little bit of that other world over with her into this one. Maybe she was saying goodbye.

Daisy held her close, rocking her, loving her in that instant way that was such a miracle. She felt it seep into every pore, every cell in her body, until she imagined she was saturated with it. A color unlike any she'd ever seen before, and so beautiful that it didn't even have a name.

"But if it takes a while to find your courage," she whispered, "forgive yourself, alright?"

The baby didn't answer. She kept sleeping, kept dreaming, her soft sounds pulling Daisy along on a ride she knew would be the most joyous one yet. This was family. This was love.

She looked up, out toward Diamond in the Rough, where the sun would be setting soon. Where Brooks and Porter would be finishing up with the guests for the night and getting ready for the dance this weekend. The barn would be dressed in her finest—tiny white Christmas lights, with stars twinkling like rhinestones overhead. It was a setting fit for the happiest of occasions, and for the first time ever, Daisy knew that she belonged there. In a home where the heart really, truly was.

She gazed down at the baby, who was just now opening her eyes. They were dark blue but would probably turn chocolate brown like her mama's.

"Your grandma would've loved you very much," Daisy

whispered. "And you know what?"

Clara blinked, her pink lips forming the cutest little heart.

"She would've told me to take my own advice."

Chapter Eighteen

Flambé in the dark for a more dramatic effect.

DAISY STOOD AT the entrance to the barn with her heart knocking against her rib cage. She'd dressed up tonight, but now felt a little silly as she watched the guests dancing and kicking the dust up in their jeans and T-shirts.

On the stage, Eddie was shredding a lime-green electric guitar, with a couple of locals playing bass behind him. He wore leather cuffs on both wrists, and his blond hair hung in sweaty strands next to his face. He was in full rocker mode tonight, singing a cover from the seventies that made her think of bell bottoms and handlebar mustaches.

He grinned when he saw her, and she waved. She still couldn't believe she was taking guitar lessons from Eddie Cole. It was just one thing on the list of many that she was having trouble wrapping her head around. Including the fact that she was back in Montana. That she was working (as a cook of all things) at Brooks's ranch. That her mother was gone… That was a hard one to believe, because she'd always thought they'd have more time.

If she'd learned anything though, it was that tomorrow wasn't a given. Nothing was promised.

She looked around. Most of the guests were dancing, thrilled with Eddie's private concert. But some of them were milling about, talking and eating the food Charlie had set out. Owen was even chatting in the corner with Eric Romano. They were both laughing, looking like whatever tension they'd brought with them from Portland had completely dissolved in the summer night. Daisy knew by now that this place had the power to do things like that. It was almost magical in a way.

Smiling, she glanced up at the Christmas lights above the stage. They twinkled merrily, reminding her that fall would be here soon. And then the holidays, bringing with them a new kind of celebration for her. A new life, lived with intention and purpose. She was so thankful for the second chance she'd been given in this little town that had started out as home, and by some miracle, had ended up that way, too. She was thankful for her sister, and the fact that she was going to be a part of her niece's life. And she was thankful for Brooks. For the way he'd believed in her when she'd had a hard time believing in herself.

But as grateful as she was, as much joy that was filling her heart tonight, she knew there was one more thing she needed to do in order to truly be at peace with whatever the future would bring. She'd opened up to Brooks a lot these last few weeks, and she'd made it pretty clear that they didn't have to get back together in order for her to love him. But she hadn't told him how she felt, how she *really* felt about him. She understood him now, in a way that she hadn't as a teenager. She knew he'd been scared of making the same mistakes his parents had, and that had been justified. She knew he'd built a wall—maybe not to keep her out, but to keep himself in, and that had been justified, too. But she'd internalized those things before, had been hurt by them. Now, they were simply pieces to his puzzle. And they were helping her understand herself better, too—her own fears and insecurities, all the things that had dictated her life up until now. Including leaving Marietta. Including leaving him.

All of a sudden, the thought that he didn't know how she felt with absolute certainty, was turning her inside out. She needed to see him, needed to talk to him. She needed to tell him that she was in love with him and wanted to try again. Life was too short to throw this away. If it didn't work, it didn't work, but at least they could say they tried, which is more than they'd done before.

She looked around again, craning her neck for any sign of him. She saw Porter over by the stage, chatting up some guests, and Charlie, who waved to her from across the barn. The older woman wore a bedazzled tank top, and jeans with a huge, sparkly belt buckle. You could see her from a mile away, like a lighthouse beacon guiding you home. Daisy grinned and waved back.

But still no Brooks.

The barn felt warm, a little too claustrophobic, so she headed outside where the stars glittered overhead. A cool breeze blew against her face as she walked over to one of the paddocks. Tilting her head back, she looked up at the stars and pulled in a deep breath.

She loved how the ranch smelled—sweet like wildflowers, tangy like animals. It smelled like the damp, rich banks of the river that flowed so darkly just beyond the midnight pastures. The moon would be reflecting on the black currents now, a dance of heaven and earth, as old as time itself.

"I've been looking for you."

Daisy startled, turning toward the sound of the deep voice behind her. And there he was. *Brooks.* Looking so handsome in a black western shirt and dark-washed Wranglers, that her heart tripped over itself at the sight.

"I've been looking for you, too," she said. "Everywhere."

He walked over, his boots scuffing the gravel. He wasn't wearing his hat tonight. Instead, his hair was combed neatly, curling in a little at the nape of his neck. He smelled clean, like he'd just showered, but he already had a shadow of stubble on his jaw. He could probably grow a beard overnight. The thick, sexy kind that belonged on lumberjacks in flannel shirts.

"Looks like we found each other," he said, stopping just close enough that she could reach out and touch him if she wanted. And she did want. More than anything.

She leaned back against the paddock fence, feeling the wood splinters through her dress. She smiled and glanced toward the barn. "It's a good party in there."

"The last nights are always fun. But a little sad. At least I think so, but maybe I'm too much of a sap."

"Are you kidding? Tall, dark, and sensitive? I'd say kill me now, but I'm already dead."

He tugged on a strand of her hair. "Don't say that. I've kind of gotten used to having you around."

"Is that so?"

"True story."

She ran her tongue over her lips, trying to find the right words. Come right out and tell him she wanted to be his girlfriend again? Seemed kind of jarring…

Her heart was beating so hard, she could almost feel the blood swishing through her veins. She could hear it, like the rush of the Marietta River underneath the summer moon.

She steeled herself. This was why she'd come tonight—to tell him how she felt. Even if it was hard, even if he didn't feel the same. She wanted to open herself up to life, and all the possibilities that came with it. That wasn't always going to be easy. Sometimes it might even break her heart.

"Brooks—"

He reached for her hand. His skin was rough, sexy. Moving over hers in a way that made everything else fade into the background.

"Don't say anything."

She looked up at him, quiet as he squeezed her fingers.

"I've been thinking," he said. "A lot, since you came home... I was still mad at you at first."

She swallowed hard. She'd known that. She'd seen it in his eyes on day one.

"But it didn't take long to get over that part," he continued. "And move right back into loving you."

Her heart had been thumping steadily, but at that, it slowed. *Loving you...*

She remembered the small piece of paper tucked inside her wallet at that very moment. Fragile and yellowing, she'd carried it with her for years. *The only real stumbling block is fear of failure. In cooking, you've got to have a what-the-hell attitude...* It was a quote from Julia Child, her mother's hero. Daisy had been afraid of a lot in the kitchen when she'd first stepped inside it. But the only thing she was afraid of tonight, was letting any more time slip away from her.

"Daisy," he said, running his knuckles across her cheek. "I just need to tell you—"

"It doesn't matter what you need to tell me."

He raised his dark brows.

"It doesn't," she said, "because I'm going to tell you something first." She took a breath and paused long enough to steady herself. "I get why you didn't want to get married right after high school."

He watched her, quiet.

"You'd been moved around so much that you didn't

know which way was up. You had a famous dad who was too busy with his career to notice. And your mother left. The one person who should've stayed no matter what."

He swallowed, his Adam's apple bobbing up and down. It seemed so simple to her right then, this final reckoning. This acknowledgment of his pain. But as a girl, she'd been so wrapped up in her own pain, that she'd been blinded to anything else. It had been a cruel cycle, repeating itself over and over again.

"I understand now, how wrong it was to give you an ultimatum about marriage. How unfair of me that was. I thought that love meant doing anything I could to keep you. When what I should've done, was love you through it. I should've given you time. I should've waited for you, Brooks."

The music from inside the barn came to a stop, and the crowd cheered and clapped, before Eddie and the band moved on to something slower, sweeter.

And still, she stood there. Asking for his forgiveness. But more than anything, granting it to herself.

"I love you," she said simply. "I've always loved you. And I always will love you. I know I work for you now, and we have a complicated history, but I want to try and—"

He put a finger to her lips and smiled. Deep dimples cutting into both cheeks. "Damn it, woman. That was supposed to be my line."

She gazed up at him.

"I was crazy to let you leave here," he said huskily, "without getting on my knees and begging you to stay. But I didn't, because in my world, that kind of devotion…"

"I get it," she said. "The only real stumbling block is fear of failure. Julia Child said that."

"Oh yeah?"

"My mom used to repeat it, over and over. I just wish we could go back. I wish we could all go back and do it over again. Do it right this time."

He wrapped an arm around her waist and pulled her close. So close that her breasts brushed against his chest, and his belt buckle bit into her hip. She could get used to his belt buckle against her hip. She could get used to a lot of things about Brooks Cole.

"We can't go back," he said. "But we still have time to fix it. You and me."

Her eyes stung. It seemed too good to be true, that they were standing here in each other's arms again. On a summer night, with live music thumping in their ears. It seemed almost like they *had* gone back in a way. Like they'd been granted a small miracle, and now there was nothing ahead of them but possibility and light.

"So, you forgive me, then?" she asked. "For leaving like I did?"

He shook his head and rubbed his thumb against the small of her back. "Honestly, I think I forgave you a long time ago. The one I've been having trouble with is me,

Daisy. And my mom…"

There was a flash in his eyes that she recognized as something between anger and pain.

"I think about her sometimes," he went on. "But it's okay. It's okay, because she taught me something."

Daisy pressed herself closer. "What's that?"

"She taught me what kind of man I want to be. And it's not the kind to turn my back on the good stuff ever again." He brushed her hair away from her face and smiled. "I guess after everything, it's just that simple. Grab life by the horns."

She smiled back. "I'm really hoping I'm the horns in this scenario."

He bent slowly, hovering over her mouth for a second. Just long enough to light a fire in her belly. To make her knees weak, and her heart pound in that way that only he could. He'd always been the one.

And then, he kissed her.

Daisy had been kissed plenty in her life. She'd been kissed by Alex, and by boys at dances whose names she couldn't remember. But this kiss…this was different. It was like the summer night they stood in, caressing something deep inside her with its warmth, its brightly burning embers. It was like the music coming from inside the old barn, the notes from the electric guitar filling her up, making her whole, making her feel alive and vibrant and full of love.

But mostly, it was like coming home again.

Epilogue

BROOKS CLOSED THE front door and took his hat off. Elvira immediately sauntered over, meowing up at him.

"I don't know what you want. I've got nothing for you."

He picked her up and plopped her in her bed on the windowsill. "There. Take a load off."

The hummingbirds of summer had thinned over the last few weeks, but the finches still came by to give her a show.

She sat on her glossy black haunches and watched one of them singing an early morning tune on the edge of a hanging basket. There was a chill in the air, the trees outside tinged with orange and gold. Fall had arrived, and the old ranch house felt cozy and warm with a small fire crackling in the fireplace. It smelled good this morning, the aroma of something baking wafting in from the kitchen. Brooks could hear Daisy humming under her breath, as she moved about shutting cupboards and running the faucet.

"I set the haybales out by the front porch," he called out to her. "Anything else you want me to do before they get here?"

"No, that's great!" she called back. "I'm going to decorate

right after I take this pie from the oven."

He smiled at that and ran a hand through his hair. She'd settled into life on the ranch like she'd been born to it. Most days she got up at dawn and fussed over the guests until well past suppertime. When she wasn't running the kitchen, she was fishing with him. Although that took a little convincing on his part, because more often than not, they'd end up skinny dipping instead.

And the cooking? Well, forget about it. She'd gotten so good at that part, there was a silky red ribbon hanging next to the stove from the county pie baking contest she'd entered in August. She'd gotten second place with her chocolate cream pie. Next year, she was determined to take first. She'd even invented a new recipe—something with pumpkin spice and nutmeg, that she'd been testing out on his dad during their weekly guitar lessons. His skinny, rock and roll father, was actually starting to develop a paunch that hung softly over his leather pants.

"Come in here!" she called.

He did as he was told and walked into the kitchen, but stopped when he saw her bending over the stove to take the pie out. She was an absolute vision—long, honey-colored hair piled high on her head, her long, slender neck begging to be kissed. She wore a brown, oversize sweater today, and a pair of faded jeans. But to him, she might as well have been wearing an evening gown. She took his breath away without even trying. Just by being Daisy.

Straightening, she set the pie on the cooling rack and blew a strand of hair away from her eyes. When she saw him, she smiled. "Hey, handsome."

"Hey, yourself."

"I just wanted to give you a kiss," she said. "To thank you for putting those haybales out. I think the kids will get a kick out of the decorations, don't you think? They're not too old for that kind of stuff?"

They were getting ready for a group of foster kids, sixth and seventh graders who were having some trouble in their home environment. They'd spend a week at Diamond in the Rough learning how to care for the animals, which in Brooks's experience, could heal just about any broken heart. On a personal level, he could relate to kids this age, since he could remember his own painful adolescence with crystal clarity. The awkwardness, the insecurity, the desperate feeling of wanting to be older, but at the same time, secretly wanting to stay little. It was a tender age, an important age, and he was looking forward to this group, maybe more than he'd looked forward to any particular group in a while.

He crossed the kitchen in a few purposeful strides. When he reached Daisy, he wrapped an arm around her waist and tilted her chin up with his fingertips so he could see into those soft brown eyes.

"No," he said. "I don't think they're too old. I think they're just right."

She looked relieved, relaxing into him in that way that

made him want to carry her off to bed. But they had work to do. He made a mental note to carry her off to bed later, though. It wouldn't be a long trip, since lately she spent more time in his room than her own.

"Oh, I hope so," she said. "I want this week to be special for them."

"It'll be special."

"And I want them to remember it."

"They'll remember it. Don't worry."

"And the menu?" she said. "Did you take a look at that?"

She had all the meals planned out, and every single one of them was full of comfort food. Chocolate chip pancakes with homemade whipped cream and fresh strawberries for breakfast. Sharp cheddar grilled cheese sandwiches with tomato basil soup for dinner. And don't even get him started on the desserts. These kids were in for quite the culinary experience. In fact, they'd probably be so preoccupied with eating, he might have some trouble getting them outside for some fun.

"I looked at it," he said, tucking a strand of hair behind her ear. "And it's perfect. Just like you."

"Ha. I know better than that."

"I think you're perfect."

"Well, now I'm falling in love with you all over again," she muttered.

"Sounds like we're in the same boat."

Tilting her head back, she gazed up at him. Her tan from

summer was fading, but her skin was still golden. Kissed by the Montana sun.

"What would you say if I asked you to marry me?" he said.

He brought it up a lot. At first it had been to test the waters. And then, he'd started picturing their wedding, *really* picturing it. Their honeymoon, their life together. Watching their kids grow up on the ranch. He was sure they'd end up having kids, one way or another. Like he kept telling her—there were lots of ways to start a family.

"I'd say we're supposed to be taking it slow, remember?"

He bent and kissed her neck, breathing in her scent. This morning, she smelled like vanilla and sugar. "We can take it as slow as you want," he murmured against her skin. "Just as long as you give in eventually."

She laughed. "You're nothing if not persistent."

"What can I say? You're worth waiting for."

At that, she reached up and wrapped her arms around his neck. He knew she wanted him to keep asking. And when the time was right, she'd say yes. He wasn't in a hurry—they had all the time in the world. For him, the hard part was over. He'd found her, lost her, and found her again. The rest was all about holding onto her this time, making sure she felt safe and loved. And cherished, above all else.

She watched him. Her eyes were big and dark, pools of warmth and emotion that he found he could look into forever. Until her blond hair turned silver, and her hands shook with age.

"My mama would say we're a slow burn, Brooks Cole."

He smiled. *Most definitely.*

And that was the very best kind.

The End

Want more? Check out Rae and Griffin's story in
Montana Christmas Magic!

Join Tule Publishing's newsletter for more great reads and
weekly deals!

If you enjoyed *Montana Rancher's Kiss,*
you'll love the next book in….

The Cole Brothers series

Book 1: *Montana Christmas Magic*

Book 2: *Montana Rancher's Kiss*
View the series here!

Book 3: *Coming August 2021!*

More books by Kaylie Newell

The Harlow Brothers series

The Harlow brothers learned at a young age that family is what you make of it. Born on the wrong side of the tracks and abandoned by their father, Judd, Luke and Tanner have grown into remarkably tough men who are jaded by life. But when they come together as guardians of their orphaned half-sister, they'll find that love is what you make of it, too. As they learn how to be the fathers they never had, their carefully constructed walls begin to crack. But it will take three strong women to tear those defenses down for good, and show them what true happiness looks like.

Book 1: *Tanner's Promise*
Book 2: *Luke's Gift*
Book 3: *Judd's Vow*

The Elliotts of Montana series

Book 1: *Christmas at Sleigh Bell Farm*
Book 2: *Betting on the Bull Rider*

Available now at your favorite online retailer!

About the Author

For Kaylie Newell, storytelling is in the blood. Growing up the daughter of two writers, she knew eventually she'd want to follow in their footsteps. She's now the proud author of over a dozen books, including the RITA® finalists, *Christmas at The Graff* and *Tanner's Promise*.

Kaylie lives in Southern Oregon with her husband, two daughters, a blind Doberman, and two indifferent cats.

Thank you for reading

Montana Rancher's Kiss

If you enjoyed this book, you can find more from all our great authors at TulePublishing.com, or from your favorite online retailer.

TULE
PUBLISHING